The Power of the Gift

THE POWER OF THE GIFT

OF THE GIFT

CHRISTOPHER MOON

POLESTAR
BOOK PUBLISHERS

Published by:
Polestar Press Ltd.
P.O. Box 69382, Station K
Vancouver, B.C.   V5K 4W6

Distributed in Canada by:
Raincoast Book Distribution Ltd.
112 East Third Avenue
Vancouver, B.C.   V5T 1C8

Edited by Wendy Bond
Cover art and design by Jim Brennan

The publishers would like to gratefully acknowledge
assistance from the British Columbia Cultural Services Branch
and the Canada Council.

Printed and bound in Canada by Best Gagne Printers

Canadian Cataloguing in Publication Data
Moon, Christopher, 1955-
  The power of the gift

ISBN 0-919591-12-4

    I. Title.
PS8576.055P6 1992   C813'.54   C92-091295-8
PR9199.3.M66P6 1992

ACKNOWLEDGEMENTS

First and foremost, I would like to thank Dr. Chuck Spezzano for much of the information and terminology in this book, as well as for his pioneering efforts in the integration of spirituality and psychology. He has cut a new path for the entire world.

Second, thank you Chuck and Lency Spezzano for saving my life. Your character and essence can be felt throughout this book.

Third, I want to acknowledge the Course in Miracles that is the foundation for much of this book's material.

Fourth, to my editor, Wendy Bond: thank you for helping me with this story. You have the gift of transforming writing into storytelling. That is one of the most valued arts in the world.

Next, to all my friends, too numerous to name here. Look closely and, somewhere in this series, you will see the inspiration you have given me to keep me honest.

Lastly, to the community of Nelson: You have welcomed and nurtured me and my family, and allowed me to see that a City of Light truly is possible.

*This book is dedicated to my
beautiful wife Su Mei, in whom the
goddess Quon Yin once again
walks the earth.*

CONTENTS

THE WARRIOR'S RESOLVE

"Go away," the man said kindly, "I have nothing to offer you."
I dropped my head and turned away, frustrated and confused.
It was my tenth visit to his tiny abode, my tenth long, arduous
drive over dirt and gravel roads to reach the secluded cottage
where Mr. Xavier resided. Ten useless trips—useless except
to my mechanic, who was quickly growing rich from my
attempts, so much so that he was even planning a luxurious
second honeymoon around my con-tinued efforts to convince
Mr. Xavier to take me on as a pupil.

But no more, I resolved firmly as I got into my Pontiac and ·
backed up along the dirt track for a quarter mile before I could
find enough space to turn around. The area was heavily
wooded, and the sunlight playing off the autumn-coloured
leaves did its best to lighten my mood, but I would have none
of it this time. After the usual hour of bump and grind, and the
loss of another piece of my car, I turned onto the highway
toward town, my gloom darkening with each passing mile. I
headed for the pub where I was sure Peter Cairn would be
waiting for his chance at my weekly razzing. After ten weeks,

it had all become part of a sordid ritual.

Since the first of August, I had visited Mr. Xavier every Monday, attracted by an ad in the Personals section of the local newspaper. Not that I made it a habit to read that stuff, mind you; it was just that I was sitting in a restaurant one morning, thinking how nice it would be to have a female companion across from me, when I happened to open the paper to the classifieds. For a laugh, I thought I'd check out the Personals to see how far the "lonely people" were going to fill the gaps in their lives.

"You got your ad in there?" Peter's voice came loudly over my shoulder and by reflex I quickly turned to the financial section.

"Hey there, Pete!" I greeted him as he squeezed his large frame into the seat across from me. "I was just thumbing through the Want Ads—see if there's a better job for me somewhere out there."

"Sure," my friend smiled knowingly, and I blushed to confirm his suspicions. "Let me have a look at them." He reached over and relieved me of the paper. As he scanned through it, I did my best to turn the heat down on my face by studiously concentrating on the menu—which I could, in fact, recite by heart. "Straight white male, N.S., S.D., not unattractive, loves sports, movies and interesting conversation. Looking for female, 25-30, not unattractive, with similar interests, et cetera, et cetera…This is yours, Kennedy, I bet you ten bucks!"

"How could you tell?" I asked meekly, the blood returning to my face.

"The 'not unattractive' part is a dead giveaway—you're the only guy in this city who would put that down. Every other guy would say that he wanted someone good looking, or beautiful, or something like that. But not you, you're too nice for that. Not unattractive—what does that mean, anyway? Man, you didn't even tell them to include a photo."

"Well, I don't want someone beautiful," I protested.

"Uh huh. Sure, and I don't want a million bucks—hell, I love being in debt!"

"No, I mean I want more than just looks," I explained lamely. Peter smiled and continued to read the ads. Our waitress arrived and we gave her our order, Peter hardly looking up to say hello. After reading aloud some of the more amusing ads, he became suddenly silent and frowned. From his eye movements I could see that he was re-reading the same section, as though he were attempting to understand a foreign language or a puzzle.

"Look at this." He handed the paper over to me, pointing to an ad that took up half a column:

> FOUND—Your Warrior's Passion. Lost some-
> where in the vicinity of your distant past. Anyone
> wishing to reclaim it, please see me A.S.A.P.

The rest of the ad gave highly complicated directions to some place out of town, up in the mountains, or at least the foothills. To follow them with any success appeared highly risky, as they relied on spotting certain old trees and oddly-shaped rock formations. At the bottom was the name G. Xavier. I looked over the strange words, and finally put the paper aside when our food arrived. "Huh! What do you think?"

"Dunno," Peter replied, putting half a sausage into his mouth. "I just wonder if anyone would be dumb enough to go all the way out there. It's either a practical joke, or else there's some crazy hermit looking for company—y'know, someone he can talk gibberish to, or drool over."

"Maybe." I was unconvinced. Something about the first line had sent a shiver down my spine. My ever-observant friend noticed immediately.

"Pat, don't even think about it," he advised. "It's too weird, even for you. For all you know, if it's for real, it could be some crazy pervert looking to rape you and then chop you into little pieces."

"Maybe," I repeated, "but what if it is for real? What if it's...I dunno...like Don Juan or something? You know, like a sorcerer or a medicine man or—"

"—or some hillbilly like in *Deliverance*," my friend finished for me.

"There aren't any hillbillies in those mountains, Pete. Not bad ones anyway—just a bunch of ex-hippies and draft dodgers."

"No bad hillbillies that we know of," he corrected me. "But anyway, this whole thing is too weird for me—I mean, what's a sorcerer or witch doctor doing, putting an ad in the newspaper? And the Personals section at that?"

"I don't know—to reach someone like me, maybe," I answered lightly, "someone sensitive, intelligent, a spiritual seeker."

"Don't forget not unattractive," he reminded me, "and also—desperate."

"Maybe," I announced with a mock look of saintly destiny, "maybe I'm *being called*." But as I spoke, I noticed that I had already lost the tingling sensation of earlier, and soon our conversation drifted to other topics, until we parted company for work.

By the end of the day, I was no longer giving it any thought, and the evening was spent at the Elk's Horn Pub, waiting for Ms. Right to enter my life, and listening to Peter's irreverent but humorous criticisms of society, politics, every patron that walked through the door, and the rest of the world. By the time I had arrived home and swooned into the lonely warmth of my bed, G. Xavier was gone from my mind.

The next morning I found the ad again. Actually, it was more like the ad finding me, as it jumped out at me as soon as I opened the paper. That same electrical vibration coursed through my body, and before Peter could show up to talk me out of it, I was driving down the highway, pumping myself up with rock and roll music and a wild metaphysical fantasy. I was going to be another Castaneda, or Lynn Andrews— maybe even a modern-day Arjuna or Milarepa! I was going to place myself in service to this G. Xavier person and learn the way of the Spiritual Warrior! I was going to walk the path of Truth…I was going to become enlightened! I was…

I was going to spend the better part of a day rattling my brains on logging roads that led nowhere. After four or five hours, I had seen more clear-cuts than most loggers see in a week, but I discovered not the least sign of human habitation. By mid afternoon I found my way back to the highway and a much-needed gas station. After filling up, I headed for home, feeling both foolish and spiritually depleted. I could already hear Peter's voice in my head, telling me that my propensity for airy-fairy ideals and daydreams would be my downfall. "Why can't you come and live in the real world? Give up this Pollyanna shit and become a responsible, productive member of the human race." Then he would pull out a joint or drop a tab of acid in his beer. To Peter, the Real World was for people who couldn't face drugs, but he loved to dole out advice, trying, he would say, to save me because it was already too late for him. The outcome of our talk would be that, once again, I was wrong.

It was at this point that I spotted it on the other side of the highway: an old logging road, marked on each side by two very tall and very dead fir trees. How had I missed it before? How could anyone miss something that obvious? Easy, for me—I was probably daydreaming as usual. More than once it had been remarked that I could miss a nuclear war if it happened right under my nose, so much did I tend to get lost in trance.

Once again I was bounced and jogged around by two more hours of searching and backtracking until, finally, I came upon the house. It was actually more like a shack, no, maybe not even that grand. The wood and moss structure seemed to grow out of the hillside that made up its east wall, and it had a dark, intimidating quality—so much so that it took me some time to work up the courage to leave my car. My overactive mind conveniently chose this time to take up Peter's suggestion, as it replayed key scenes from *Deliverance* and *Southern Comfort*, films about city folk being hunted down and tortured or killed in gory fashion by crazy, inbred mountain folk. Looking at the shack, I began to imagine the haunting sound of a banjo permeating the deceptively peaceful forest. Finally I left my car, placing my trusty baseball bat on the passenger seat, locking three doors, and leaving the driver's side open. Sweating profusely in the warm evening air, I approached the hovel.

He appeared promptly after my first knock, a middle-aged man, about five-foot-six, brown hair, a clean-shaven leathery face, and the kindest, deepest blue eyes I have ever seen. There was only darkness behind him, since the shanty had no windows.

"Yes?" His voice was gentle, neither deep nor high, and he smiled openly as he buttoned up his red and black plaid shirt. Then, "Oh—it's you, is it?" as though he recognized me but had only half-expected me to show up.

"Hi," I said, uncertainly, shuffling my feet uncomfortably with the sudden urge to go pee.

"What can I do for you?"

"Well, uh…I read your notice in the paper today—well, yesterday and today actually, and, uh…well, I'm not sure what to say, but…uh…it sort of gave me the feeling that I should…uh…well, that I should meet you, and talk to you about it."

"About what?" His voice was melodious, seeming to be a part of the air and the sounds around us: the rustling leaves and creaking trees, the occasional bird or squirrel chattering. Soon I was feeling a little more relaxed.

"About what you said in the paper—about my passion."

"What about it?"

"Well, I thought you could help me get back my passion for life," I blurted out quickly, surprised at the desperation in my voice. The man's eyes pierced into mine and I froze, feeling self-conscious and not knowing whether to meet his gaze or look away. After a long silence he finally spoke, and I could breathe again.

"Go away—I have nothing to teach you." Without another word he turned back into his hovel and I was left staring at the weathered plywood door. After awhile I turned back to my vehicle and drove away, dazed and confused. When I related the story to Peter he simply shrugged and said, "Takes all kinds," and then went on to discuss other items of interest, more pertinent to the real world. But it was not that easy for me. I could not get my mind off the man's face nor forget those eyes that had stared at me with such intensity and yet with so much laughter. Not even when I had been in the grip of the most obsessively romantic feelings for a woman did I see eyes that danced the way Mr. Xavier's had—without actually moving.

After a restless night, I was somewhat relieved to pick up the paper the next morning and discover that his curious ad was no longer printed. In a few days the restlessness subsided, replaced by the stimulation of some surprising developments. My personal ad was receiving attention. By Thursday, just three days after it first appeared, I had received seven responses.

"What d'you expect—that 'not unattractive' crap left it open for anyone to answer," Peter was kind enough to explain to me, but I was riding the high that comes when a door that has long been barred suddenly opens wide. By Friday I had a total of fifteen replies to consider and I felt like a teenager at his first school dance. I spent the evening by myself, reading and re-reading each correspondence, scrutinizing them with the kind of near-paranoid suspicion that over five years in the counselling profession had given me. It was my intent to weed out anyone who gave away any impression that they might be more neurotic than I was. I tried categorizing them in different ways, from handwriting style to the colour of ink used. Then I gathered them up and separated them according to artistic preferences, profession, activities, age, sense of humour, and intelligence. After resisting the temptation to throw them all out and start drinking heavily, I decided to choose the five best on the basis of individuality. That was a laugh! Each corre-spondent had a unique way of expressing what they had to offer, but between the lines was a recurring theme of the same unmet needs that I had. Damn! I said mentally to these women, did you ever get the wrong number! We're all in the same boat.

It was then that I noticed among the pile of discarded envelopes, a smaller one, still unopened. As I handled it pensively, the wonderful scent of gardenia wafted up to my nose and I was overtaken by an unreasonable hope. Tearing it open, I was stunned to see the ad pasted onto a piece of paper:

> FOUND—Your Warrior's Passion. Lost some-where in the vicinity of your distant past. Anyone wishing to reclaim it, please see me A.S.A.P.

Suddenly the other letters seemed so unimportant, even ludicrous, as Xavier's eyes reappeared in my mind. I could not even attempt to meet any of those women until I had something to offer them. Otherwise, I was sure, it would turn out to be a rerun of my marriage, with me playing beggar at the rich woman's door. I just didn't have what it takes: the confidence, the passion, the sense of self...I was a hollow shell. I knew that I had to talk to Xavier again. I had to tell him of my lifelong dissatisfaction with the world; of how empty and fruitless all my pursuits were. Surely he would see how sincerely I wanted to know the purpose of my life, and how important the Truth was to me. If anyone would understand,

I was certain that he would. He had to take me on as his pupil, no matter what I had to do to convince him. I would sit on his doorstep and prove my sincerity until he accepted me. He had to make me his pupil!

"What makes you so sure he wants a pupil—I didn't see anything about that in the ad, did you?" Peter asked. It was Saturday, and I was on the road again, looking for the dead fir trees that marked the entrance to my destiny. This time Peter accompanied me, to prove to himself, he said, that I really was as stupid as I was pretending to be.

"It's just a feeling I have," I told him. "It's like I'm being called, or something."

"Hey look, P.K., I read the same metaphysical stuff you did, remember? I was the one who loaned you all the Don Juan and Rolling Thunder books. I was the guy that got those Ram Dass tickets the first time he came here—remember?"

"Yeah, I remember. So what's your point—did I forget to say thanks or something?"

"No, I'm just saying that maybe they went to your head a little too much. I think you're putting your own interpretation onto that thing in the newspaper."

"But this guy's real," I reminded him. "He talked to me."

"Yeah, and he told you to beat it. He didn't say anything about being a teacher, or a master or anything; he's just some crazy old fart who likes to screw around with naive types like you."

"Thanks for the vote of confidence, buddy."

"I'm just a concerned friend—you know how I worry about you, man. I hate to see you go off the edge like this. Your mom always said you had an overactive imagination—remember?"

"Yeah, I remember. She said it every day—almost as often as she told me not to hang around with you, that you were a bad influence."

"Great men are always misunderstood. Especially by their friends' mothers." Peter sighed like a long-suffering saint, and put a hand to his forehead.

"I just wish this road were part of my imagination," I said as we bumped along the trail. "I'm going to lose my muffler one of these times."

When we reached the shack, I approached it with a

gnawing dread in my gut. After repeated knocks on the door and Peter's irreverent hoots and yodels, it became evident that the man was not home. "Where the hell would a guy like that go, anyway?" my friend wondered. "It's not like there's a lot in the way of entertainment out here. What would a guy like that do with his time?"

"I dunno. Maybe he's out collecting berries or something. Or talking to some animals...."

"What would anyone have to say to an animal? How much is there to say to a deer or a coyote anyway? I'd imagine that your conversation would be extremely limited, wouldn't you think?"

"Maybe he's meditating."

"Maybe he's gone to a movie," Peter countered. "I know I would if I was livin' out here—I'd be spending a lot of time at the movies. Just look at this dump!"

"Yeah, well, he should show up here some time today," I stated halfheartedly.

"I'll just take the car and leave you here then, shall I?"

"What?" I asked, taken aback.

"Sure," my friend explained, "Aren't you just going to camp out on his doorstep and wait to prove what a sucker— I mean, what a sincere seeker of truth you are?"

"But he might not come back! What's the use of proving something to someone who ain't even here? It gets cold out here at night y'know."

"Oh ye of little faith." He smirked. "C'mon, let's get the hell outta here."

"Well...okay," I conceded with only a hint of hesitation. "But I'm coming back out here on Monday."

"How do you know this guy's got anything to offer you anyway?" Peter continued to prod me as we drove to town. "He told you he didn't—how does that make him a spiritual teacher? Christ, anyone could have sent you that ad in the mail, knowing the clowns you have for friends."

"You're one of my friends," I reminded him.

"Exactly—see what I mean?"

"I can't explain it. I just have a feeling this is important for me."

"If you say so. I just can't see how a guy who lives in a rat hole like that can have anything to teach anybody."

"One way or another I'm going to find out," I announced determinedly. "I'm just going to keep on trying." And so I did, returning to the old shack every Monday, beseeching the enigmatic Mr. Xavier to take me under his spiritual wing. Every week, I asked him in a different way—to teach me the truth, to show me the purpose of life, to show me who I am, to initiate me onto the path of enlightenment. Once I even asked him to show me how to meet my soul mate, but although he met that request with a hearty laugh, his replies varied little over the weeks that passed. "I can't teach you anything...go away, I have nothing to give to you...leave me alone, I am of no use to you..."

"Well," Peter stated cheerfully as he patted me on the back, "I give you full points for courage and determination, Patrick! Or is it stupidity and bullheadedness—it's so hard to tell with you."

"I don't get it," I said dejectedly. "What do I have to do to prove myself to that bastard? It's been ten friggin' weeks I've been going out there. What does he want from me?"

"Kennedy, did you ever consider that the guy's maybe a bit nuts? All things considered, there's not much about this situation that's what you'd call normal, y'know. Why don't you just give this up; don't keep on letting this guy string you along. Whatever happened to the Patrick Kennedy whose sole aim in life was to find Miss Perfect and screw his brains out?"

"I dunno," I responded. "It just all started to seem so useless...so hopeless."

"So that's it! You're using this little weekly crusade of yours as an excuse not to feel like a failure with women. C'mon man, you're a great guy! You'd be a big gift for any woman—hell, I'd marry you myself if you didn't have such a hairy chest. You just need a little more confidence is all, believe me, man. Forget that jerk in the rat hole and get on with your life."

"Get on with my life," I said thoughtfully. "What the hell does that mean anyway? I don't feel like I've ever had a life of my own to get on with—just stuff I do to please other people, most of whom I never see. Have you ever seen society, Peter? Actually seen it? What is it anyway? I spend a lot of time trying to live by its codes and fit into its standards, but I've never actually met society. We're all members of this great big club and we spend most of our lives living for it, but we don't even know anything about it: where it came from, why it's here or why we live to please it. Okay, so maybe what I'm doing with this Xavier fellow isn't exactly normal or socially acceptable, but I'll tell you something: a lot of the time that I spent chasing girls, and then women, I was doing it because that's what I thought I was supposed to do. To be a man, or just to be considered normal. Sure I've wanted a relationship, but it was mainly because I thought it would cure my loneliness. Ever since this Xavier thing started, I've realized that that was society's way to cure it. Man, I didn't even know what I wanted. Even if Xavier is a total flake, I'm learning more from my stupidity than I ever did from society's wisdom." After I finished speaking, Peter turned away and for a long time simply stared into his beer while I marvelled at the novelty of a particular feeling that I found inside of me. Although it was quite alien to me, I did recognize that it was a sense of clarity, which gave me a feeling of peace. I had no idea what I was clear about, but it was nice to know of its existence. At length, Peter Cairn got up from his seat, gently put his hand on my shoulder and smiled softly.

"Wait for me on Monday; I want to go with you," he said.

"Oh, it's you again, is it? What do you want this time?" It may have been my imagination, but Mr. Xavier seemed perturbed on this, my eleventh, visit. You couldn't tell by his eyes as he considered both Peter and myself—they had that same dancing, amused quality to them. For some reason I realized this was my last chance, that I had to say the right thing or I would never see this man again, so I hesitated to answer. What did I want anyway? I could have named off a million things that I wanted, but something was gnawing at me: were any of them what I really, *really* wanted? Did I ever in my life know enough about myself to truly know not only what I wanted but what was rightfully mine to have? How could I know what I wanted if I didn't even have a clue as to who I really was? My shoulders dropped in defeat and I would have walked away right then if not for the overwhelming despair that kept me rooted to the spot.

"Well?" Xavier demanded gently, "What do you want?"

"I'm sorry," I almost whispered the words, "I don't know what I want." The man studied me for perhaps twenty seconds, his face an inscrutable mask, and I felt like time had stopped and the world was melting into nothingness.

"Finally. Now I can teach you something!" Xavier exclaimed, and he sounded relieved, maybe even grateful. He handed me a business card. "Meet me at this address tomorrow night at seven—don't be late." I read the number on the card. It was no more than three or four houses from where I lived.

"Hey, this is right on my street!"

"I know. It's a nice neighborhood, isn't it?"

"Don't you live out here, though?"

"What—in this rat hole? What would I want to live here for?"

"Why'd I have to come all the way out here for the last three months?"

"Good question," the man replied. "But answer me this one first—Why did you have to come all the way out here for the last three months?"

"That's easy," Peter piped in, "Kennedy does everything the hard way—it's the only way he figures he can learn anything. He has to earn it."

"There's your answer," and the man chuckled. I did my best to look confused, hoping he would elaborate, but he just laughed harder. "Tomorrow night, seven o'clock sharp. Be on time."

"Can I come too?" Peter blurted brashly.

"Sure," Xavier replied, and it was all I could do not to splutter out some indignant protest. My new teacher regarded me with a smile.

"To each his own," he explained simply.

I was quiet on the drive back and merely shrugged when Peter offered to buy me a beer. We sat in silence for the first round, but Cairn never could last long sitting quietly. He began to poke and dig and pry, urging me to let him in on the reason for my taciturn behaviour. I held out stubbornly until he threatened to submit me to one of his devastating headlocks, at which point I relented.

"It's just not fair. I did all the work, and as usual you cheated your way in."

"How did I cheat?" my friend protested.

"Hell, I gave you the password!"

"What password?"

"I don't know."

"Then how do you know that you gave it to me?"

"No, 'I don't know' was the password. I've been going out there for three months trying to get him to take me in, and all that time you've just been sitting here, laughing at me and getting stoned. Or drunk. Or both. And the one time you meet the guy, he lets you in—after I did all the work! It isn't fair."

"Hey, don't worry, P.K. You're taking this whole thing too seriously."

"And you don't think this is serious?"

"I don't even know what this is all about."

"What did you ask to come along for?"

"I dunno," Peter replied with a glint in his eye, "to meet girls, maybe?"

"What?"

"Sure. Maybe this Xavier guy is running some kind of cult or something. If that's the case, you'll need someone to cover your back—you being so naive and all. And if he really is decent, maybe he's got a following. That usually means there'll be some nice ladies looking for love. If that's the case, then I came to the right spot!"

"You're not serious," I said half-questioningly.

"Why not?"

"Peter, this is important to me, man. I'm trying to do something for myself. I'm trying to…I dunno…find out about *me*…to improve my life."

"So am I, Patrick. Good sex always works wonders in my life."

"Pete, this is spirituality we're talking about."

"Sex ain't spiritual?" he challenged.

"No! I mean sure it is, but not like that. I mean, sometimes it's…" my voice trailed off weakly.

"As long as you're clear about it, Kennedy, I'm convinced. Look, neither of us knows what we're getting into. You think it'll make you into some kind of spiritual warrior—whatever the hell that is—and if it does, then great! But just by meeting that guy today, I can tell you it ain't going to be like anything you might expect. I want to leave all my options open is all. You just better let go of any ideas about how it should be, 'cause you'll only be disappointed. Drink up."

"How come you know so much about this stuff, anyway?" I asked suspiciously.

"Hey," my friend replied in his best Jack Nicholson voice, "I'm a goddamn spiritual wonder of the world, Doc." We drank for awhile in silence, both, I think, contemplating the next day's possibilities. At length, Peter looked at me seriously and said, "I don't know about you, Kennedy, but I get the feeling that the floor of my world is about to fall away from my feet. Either that or you've been spiking my beer."

"Now this is more like a house," Peter stated as we looked on the great stone structure that took up a full two lots. Until we read the name plate on the door, I had always assumed that the building had gone the way of most semi-mansions in the neighborhood; that is, subdivided and rented out to people who disliked apartments, but could not afford to buy a house. People like me. He opened the door and, smiling, waved us into a small cozy study with three overstuffed but comfortable chairs and a love seat. We each took a chair and I gazed around at the Victorian decor.

"Now what might you two be resisting?" he asked cheerfully as he took the third chair facing us.

"Nothing that I know of," Peter answered.

"Me neither. I've been looking forward to this," was my reply.

"You're four minutes late," Xavier noted.

"We're sorry, we're always late," Pete explained. "For us, this is actually early."

"I see."

"I'm really sorry," I said, feeling suddenly full of guilt. "I'll be on time next time, I promise."

"Nothing to feel bad about—it's your first lesson. Being late is just a form of resistance to your learning process. It's also your way of sending out a message to people that you can't be trusted. Besides being purely disrespectful, of course."

"Yeah," I said sheepishly, "You're right—I'm really sorry."

"Couldn't it be that it's maybe just a habit we got into?" Peter inquired.

"Yes, and where did the habit come from?"

"I dunno. I've always been late for everything ever since I can remember."

"So if you don't know where the habit came from, you don't really know where it will take you, either. Have you ever heard the saying: 'Sow a thought—reap an action, sow an action—reap a habit, sow a habit—reap a character, sow a character—reap a destiny'? No need to get into any kind of guilt trip about it; just be aware of your process. The key to everything I'm going to teach you is accountability. Learn to be personally responsible for what goes on in your life—for everything that goes on—and you can regain what you thought you'd lost forever. Be responsible for your tardiness and your awareness will put you back in touch with the greater aspect of yourself that you gave up when you chose the habit instead."

"Yeah, well, I'm sorry," I repeated, "and it won't happen again, I promise."

"Sure it will, Pat," Xavier replied in good humour, "or else you'll just have to find some other hook to hang your guilt on. Look, being responsible doesn't mean being guilty. It means being able to respond. That calls for an openness which blame, guilt, and judgement don't provide. You think that being guilty and apologizing is what makes you a good person. But it just keeps you stuck."

"Christ, Xavier, if we didn't have our guilt, all of society would be in a state of chaos!" Peter objected. "We'd all be running around doing whatever the hell we wanted."

"My God, we couldn't have that!" Xavier feigned shock.

"You know what I mean. We have enough problems with crime and violence the way things are. If we didn't have a conscience to keep us from being bad, the whole world would go nuts robbing and killing each other."

"You don't have a very high opinion of your fellow man,

do you? But before we get into a philosophical debate, let's take one thing at a time. For now, do your best to be on time and, if you're late, just ask yourself what it is that you might be resisting."

"Yeah, well it really won't happen again, I promise," I stated as sincerely as I could, hampered by a strange feeling that I was lying through my teeth.

"Now, let's start with the first of the Warrior's principles, shall we?"

"Uh," Peter interjected, "Are we the only ones coming tonight? I mean, aren't there any other…uh…students?"

"Students—you mean women, don't you? Ahh, a man after my own heart. At the moment, Peter, the others have gone on. You may catch up with them, or there may be others behind who will catch up with you. Who knows? But for now at least, there's just us three. Now then, are you ready for the first principle?"

"Sure," we responded in unison, then I added, "please." I braced myself for the impact. My life was about to change.

"Don't," the man spoke slowly and solemnly, "put off 'til tomorrow what you can do today." There was a long silence as he sat back and observed our reactions. I, for one, was stupefied. I'd been had. I had just wasted three months of my life chasing another stupid fantasy, wasting more precious time on some eccentric individual who was either misguided or just plain simple. How could I have been so stupid as to expect some wild transcendental, or at least hallucinogenic, experience to sweep me out of this world and into a place of magic and miracles? Let's face it—that kind of thing only happens in books, if at all, and only to a very few people. People like Andrews or Castaneda got to fly, or go on magical journeys. Harner got to travel in other worlds. People like me get to sit in middle-class studies and be reminded that a stitch in time saves nine! I couldn't believe it. Don't put off 'til tomorrow what you can do today?

"Gimme a break," Peter muttered.

"You're not impressed?" the man inquired innocently.

"Hardly."

"No offence, Xavier," I jumped in politely, "It's just that we were looking for something a little…well, I dunno…deeper, I guess."

"A little." Peter's voice fairly dripped with understatement. "My grandmother used to tell us that when I was a kid."

"Too bad you didn't listen to her; you could be on your way to the second principle—where the ladies are waiting. One of the major problems in both your lives is procrastination. Warriors never procrastinate. They know what is important, what their priorities are, and they handle them as they come up. Saves them lots of energy."

"Yeah, but what's that got to do with...?"

"How old would you say I am, Patrick?"

"I dunno, maybe forty-three, forty-four."

"I'd say forty-one," Peter guessed.

"I'll be sixty-nine in another month."

"Bullshit!" Peter declared, then quickly added, "I mean, you're kidding, right?"

"No kidding, Peter. I could easily prove it to you, but I prefer that you take me at my word. I actually look much younger now than I did in my mid-forties. And although I'm careful about diet and exercise, I'm not all that careful. Believe it or not, a major factor in my physical state is that I stopped putting off to another time what I could do immediately. Procrastination wastes a lot of vital energy. Look at the energy of a five- or six-year-old child—they can outlast Olympic athletes, just playing in their own back yards. Where does all that vitality come from, and where does it go?"

"People get old," Cairn suggested philosophically. "It happens."

"That's a good example of an irresponsible statement—thank you, Peter." The teacher smiled and walked over to an easel standing to the right of his chair. With a blue marker he made a small dot on the paper. "This is the starting point of any issue that comes up in your life, to be resolved or completed. It has a purpose for its existence, and carries its own particular brand of energy. If you try to ignore it, or put it aside, you're blocking a flow, thereby causing pressure to build up inside of you. If you start the project and don't complete it—" at this he drew a half circle, then let the pen drop away, "—you start losing energy like this. If, however, you start and complete the issue to your satisfaction (he drew a complete circle), then you actually gain a lot more energy to meet your next opportunity. But if you have a lot of half circles or total blocks, your vitality will either be trapped or bled off—whatever, you just don't have the 'oomph' that is rightfully yours. Procrastinators are great at creating interference in their lives."

"Interference to what?"

"To your personal power, Mr. Kennedy! To your passion!" He reached under his chair and pulled out a couple of pads and pens. "Here, take these and make a list of all the incompletes in your life—everything, large and small, that you've been putting off dealing with. Also, put an asterisk beside each of those activities that you're in the habit of putting off. I'll give you about half an hour, so take your time and really be thorough." He left the room and, after exchanging 'what the hell' shrugs, we applied ourselves to the task at hand. The first thing that popped into my mind was that light bulb in the hallway that I'd been meaning to replace for the last, let me see…my god, it must be a month, now! The rest of the list began to flow effortlessly: the books I kept meaning to return*, the letters to be written*, the articles that some magazine editors were still waiting for*, the dishes piling in the sink*, the monthly bills*, the dentist appointment**, the phone calls to return*…the list went on and on, and I noticed that I was tiring, mentally and physically, the more I wrote. As each item of unfinished business popped into mind, I felt myself shrink from the thought of 'having to do it.'

Two full pages and a half hour later, Garth Xavier re-entered the room and I handed him my paper, feeling more than a little ashamed. When my friend handed his in, I was quite surprised by the look on his face; it took a lot to get Peter to blush. The teacher looked over both our lists, and then handed them back to us.

"That's a good start. When you go home, you can finish them."

"You mean I missed something?" I inquired incredulously.

"You've barely scratched the surface. These are all items that have to be attended to, but you didn't reach the really important stuff."

"Like what kind of important stuff?"

"Did you ever ask yourself why you always put everything off 'til the last possible moment?"

"Yeah," Peter replied belligerently, "Because all this stuff sucks."

"Well then, why do you have it in your lives?"

"Hey man, shit happens—what can you do?"

"Another good example of an irresponsible statement—thank you again, Peter."

"Look," my friend persisted, "I didn't 'create' mortgages or bills, or work. These things are a fact of life—if I want to live in this society, then I've got to pay my dues. Doesn't mean that I have to like it, does it?"

"Okay," the teacher responded agreeably, "That was spoken like a true rebel. So you put off paying your dues as a way to get back at the system. Now, suppose there's a deeper reason for putting things off. What does it allow you not to do?"

"I dunno, I don't get what you mean."

"Everything, absolutely everything that happens in our life has a purpose. As human beings we are motivated solely by purpose; the question is, whose purpose—our ego's or some other part of our selves? You procrastinate—and by the look of all these asterisks, it's a way of life for both of you—because it either allows you to do something, or it makes it unnecessary for you to do something, or both. You put things off, and this allows you to give the system the finger, and what you don't have to do is...?"

"Anything else." I blurted out.

"Like what?" the teacher encouraged me.

"Like anything. I mean, if someone calls me up, I have all these things to do, so I can say I'm too busy to talk or to get together."

"Yeah," Pete joined in. "Or if someone needs my help and I don't feel like doing anything, all of a sudden I have all these unfinished jobs around the house to take care of."

"And what else?" Xavier asked. We came up with a number of responses, including some pretty outrageous points, such as putting off something important so that we could justify delaying the less important issues until the big one was taken care of.

"Good!" Garth congratulated us. "Now do you see a common thread through all these reasons?"

"Yeah—we're both lazy bums," Peter suggested.

"Even the laziness has a purpose; it gives you a sense of

control over your lives—and keeps you out of commitment."

"Ugh!" my friend protested, grabbing his stomach, "he said the 'C' word!"

"And I'm not talking about day-to-day activities and obligations—I'm talking about a lack of commitment to yourselves. As long as your head is full of all these things that you're putting off, you don't even have to think about yourselves. When was the last time either of you was a priority in your own life?"

"What do you mean—I'm always looking out for old number one here," Cairn declared proudly.

"Really?" Xavier raised an eyebrow. "Okay, I want you two to make another list—this one of all your priorities. Write them down first, then number them according to their level of importance."

"What, you mean like our responsibilities and goals, and stuff like that?" Peter asked. I noticed that he had unconsciously raised his hand like he was back in grade school.

"Whichever activities, goals or pursuits are of greatest importance to you. Just take your time and write down whatever comes to you." So saying, he walked out of the room, leaving us to our work. This time, my list did not come out as smoothly or quickly. It was a struggle to identify each item as a priority, but after a while I managed to fill a half page. On it was my work, reading, exercise, my two night school courses in Psych, homework, seeing my daughter when I could, friends, and keeping my work and living spaces in order. Looking over the page, I realized that many of the items were also on my list of incompletes—and most had asterisks beside them. Finishing first, I looked over at Pete's. He was just finishing up a slightly shorter list than mine, and it read:

> Get high #2
> Eat good food #3
> Drink good beer #2b
> Get laid #1
> Work—make lots of money #4
> Get a relationship #5
> Get laid #6

"You've got 'get laid' twice on there," I informed him.
"I like getting laid," he informed me back, then looked

briefly at my list and said, "You forgot to number yours." I
returned to my chair and was putting my last number down
when Garth walked in. He studied our pads briefly.

"Good," he commented, "I can see we've got our work cut
out for us, men."

"What d'you mean?" Peter challenged him, "I think I'm
doing pretty good for myself by the looks of my list."

"Well," the teacher looked at him evenly, and then at me,
"together your lists are two sides of the same coin. Patrick,
yours reads like some tragic tale of sacrifice and thankless
work. What do you do for a living anyway?"

"I'm a counsellor—in the private sector. I work with
personal and relationship problems."

"Do you ever have time for your own? Just looking at this
list, I get the feeling you're so busy trying to take care of other
people's problems that you keep forgetting to deal yourself
into the game. This list reeks of sacrifice. Do you spend a lot
of time worrying, by any chance?"

"What do you mean?"

"About how other people feel, about whether you're
doing what you're supposed to be doing to make them feel
better, about whether you're doing a good enough job for
them, about what they think of you, what you wear, how you
look...if your friends still like you, if they're going to stop
liking you when they see the 'real you'...but little of this takes
you into consideration. Except for the visits with your
daughter, possibly, I don't see anything that you do for you."

"What about the exercise and reading, and time with my
friends?" I argued, wondering how he could get all that from
a couple of lines. "That's all for me."

"Don't misunderstand me, Patrick. I'm not criticizing
these activities. But correct me if I'm wrong: when you're
exercising, aren't you really somewhere else in your mind?
When you're with your friends, how much of that time is
personally fulfilling and how much of it is merely distraction,
designed to keep your adrenalin pumping? Aren't most of
these items really intended just to fill up your day, while the
real you is kept locked up in a monastery? Even your visits
with your little girl, which I'm sure you treasure; I bet you
make yourself pay for them by fighting with your ex-wife for
a week before you see her. Do you see how much you feel

you have to *work* to earn your place here?"

"Hey!" Peter exclaimed, "This guy must have been reading your mail—he's got your whole life down to a 'T'." I didn't reply, but simply sat still, while my face tried on different shades of red.

"Actually, Peter, you do the same thing Patrick does, but in an opposite way. Where Patrick virtually leads the life of a monk, you've become a classic indulger. All this indulgence in drugs, alcohol and casual sex are just covers for your unwillingness to receive anything from life."

"What's wrong with sex and getting high?" Peter had his pat argument ready. "It's a natural instinct in humans to get stoned and screwed—it's only the bullshit religions that try to control people by making it wrong to be natural."

"There's nothing 'wrong' with it. All indulgences are simply habits that keep life from surprising you. Not only that, but indulgences are actually a reaction to the sacrifice you really feel you're making to this world."

"I don't sacrifice for anybody," Cairn stated proudly.

"I don't mean to burst your balloon," the teacher said calmly, "but anyone who is not living according to what's true for them, according to their highest potential, or is not at least learning to do so, is in sacrifice. You're a man of great vision, Peter, but you're not living it." As he spoke, I wondered why I was not taking offense at his casual manner of criticizing us. There was something about him that made it easy to accept. There seemed to be no malice in him.

"Believe it or not, it all comes down to how you look at the world. Deep down, you both feel like victims of it—like you were somehow abandoned on this big hostile planet, left to fend for yourselves."

"Well, all my past experience tells me that's a pretty fair assessment of our situation," Peter said.

"And, evaluating it thus, you naturally come up with a way to handle your situation. Patrick's life becomes one big apology for being here, working hard and trying to please everybody so that he can prove his usefulness, while Peter follows the dog-eat-dog approach and takes up a lot of space, doing what he wants to do, the way he wants to do it, and challenging anybody to prove that he doesn't have a right to be here. But neither of you is doing what you really want, or living the life you want to live."

"All I'm saying is that your activities, habits and patterns reflect an attitude of loyalty to the external and, meanwhile, the internal you is starving. You're both reacting to the world as if you are at effect to it. You look at the world and say, 'this is the way life is, so this is how I'm going to handle it.' But according to one of the principles of the Warrior, you are not at effect to the world. Your situation is causal. Patrick, by the very fact that you go out of your way to please the world, you have to continue to see the world as lacking and unstable; so it's your attitude that creates the world you see."

"And Peter, it's your attitude of taking whatever you can get while you can get it, and piss on everybody else, which turns this world into a jungle. But only at the expense of sacrificing the truly gifted giant that you are."

"Man!" Peter looked over at me, "This guy goes straight for the jugular—looks like he's been in both our mailboxes." I shrugged helplessly and Xavier continued.

"What you lack is the Warrior's Resolve. A true warrior knows that he or she is the priority. True warriors don't second themselves to the world; they're resolute in their determination not to give in to either sacrifice or indulgence, and they look at the world as an affect of their attitudes and perceptions. As Warrior initiates, it would further you to entertain the possibility that what you see is what you *choose* to see."

"The Warrior's Resolve does not allow for procrastination on any level; warriors go straight for what's true and they don't leave any unfinished business in their wake. Look at your list of incompletes. You haven't even touched on your unfinished business with past relationships, or all the buried guilt around your family issues. Instead of dealing with them, you try to forget their existence, or pay off the guilt through your hard work and sacrifice, without ever confronting it. But you only lose yourselves in that shuffle, so that by the time you deal out the cards, you don't even give yourselves a hand to play. You're not even in the game."

"Wow!" Peter exclaimed, genuinely impressed, "I just wish I could understand half of what you're saying. It sounds true enough, but I'm not quite getting it. My past is in the past. I don't waste time dwelling on it 'cause it's over. And sure, there's a lot of stuff I wish hadn't happened, but it's not unfinished business as far as I'm concerned. It's over."

"Just because you don't think about it, or don't feel all that much when you do think about it, doesn't mean it isn't affecting your life. I've spent a lot of time rummaging through the files of the subconscious mind—mine and other people's—and I've found that one thing keeps popping up: as far as the subconscious is concerned, whatever wasn't resolved in the past is still going on, directly affecting what is happening to you today." He paused to look at us both. Then, "You don't believe me, right? Don't worry about it—just stick around. We're only getting started; it gets a whole lot hotter! Which brings us to the subject of my fee."

"Huh?" I grunted, then recovered politely, "I mean, pardon?"

"If you want to pursue this course, it will cost you sixteen thousand dollars. The length of the course will be at least eight months, but it can be extended at my discretion."

"Jeez," I said, "I didn't know that. I thought…I mean, I really didn't understand about the money. I'm sorry."

"You mean you thought that this was all for free?"

"No, I didn't really think about it. I just assumed that it would be by donation or something like that—it being a spiritual sort of thing."

"Spiritual? Who said anything about it being spiritual?"

"What would you call it? Metaphysical, or New Age, or…what?"

"I don't know," Garth responded innocently, "I never thought about a name for it. I don't even know what 'it' is."

"Shit," Peter declared, "I never heard of Don Juan or those other guys charging money for teaching their pupils. With a house and property this size, what do you need the money for?" I shrunk from my friend's direct, brash manner, but it didn't faze Garth. He looked as though he rather enjoyed it.

"For one thing," he explained, "to maintain a house this size. But what difference does it make what I do with the money? Maybe I give it all to Mother Teresa, or maybe I stuff it in my mattress. If you don't want to pay me that kind of money, I understand perfectly. I wish you well in your life, and I'm truly glad we met—you're both really great company. But think about this: if you do take this course, not having the faintest idea what you'll be learning, it will be one of the few things that you've done for yourself for no other reason than because something inside you wanted to. No explanations, no guarantees. Just some voice inside guiding you, like it guided you to that shack. If that same voice directs you to take this course, take it. If it tells you to go elsewhere, then by all means, follow that. Because if you can't trust your own inner voice, what can you trust?"

"I didn't hear no voice," Peter objected.

"Actually, neither did I," I agreed.

"Well then, I guess I was wrong," Xavier announced cheerfully. "Our next class is Saturday morning at ten. If you're coming, bring your first two thousand dollar payment; if not, happy trails! But at least remember the Warrior's Resolve: be determined to make yourself the priority in your life, and be willing to receive all that life has to offer."

I spent a long restless night tossing and turning between logical assertiveness and emotional confusion, and the next day was neither satisfactory nor productive. I felt guilty for taking my clients' money when I was hardly there, catching only half of what they said. Occasionally my secretary would take pains to point out some serious oversight on my part, only to be rewarded with a biting rebuke that, later, I could not believe I had made. I spent the last two hours huddled in my office, so paralyzed with guilt and shame that I could not go out and face her, even at the expense of straining my bladder. I even entertained the insane hope that she would up and quit, saving me the embarrassment of ever having to deal with her again.

At first glance, it seemed that Peter had not fared much better. When I met him at the Elk's Horn that night, he looked to be well on his way to Booze Heaven, chugging them back the way he was. When I took a closer look, his eyes betrayed the signs of drug use. "How you doing?" I asked him.

"Great—and you?"

"The shits."

"Well then, all systems are normal."

"Yeah. What happened last night, anyway?"

"Beats the hell out of me." Peter's speech was not slurred nor his manner uncoordinated, in spite of his intoxication. "Y'know Kennedy, I like sex. I must think about beautiful women, or look at them, at least ninety percent of the day. And

I dream about it, too. Along with making money and getting high, sex is where I'm at in life."

"Is this supposed to be news to me?" I inquired.

"Last night that guy tore my whole life apart as if it were just so much garbage. Everything I live for—he tells me that it's all a pile of dung."

"You seemed pretty impressed by it at the time, man. I didn't hear you arguing a whole lot—not like you usually do."

"I was too busy enjoying his smooth talking to realize he was cutting me down," my friend admitted.

"Yeah, well I was okay with it 'til he brought up the part about the money. Hell, they don't even charge that much for a whole year of university. And it's not like he's got any big fantastic trip. I know my life is screwed; how's changing a light bulb and doing my dishes going to help that? Sixteen thousand dollars to be told not to put off 'til tomorrow what I can do today; what's our next lesson—the early bird catches the worm?"

"We'll find out on Saturday, won't we?"

"What!" I spluttered, "You're not going back there, are you?"

"Of course—aren't you?"

"For sixteen thousand bucks? No friggin' way! Why would you go back? It's not like you're going to trip out on some Shamanic stuff or play with altered states. It'll be like eight months of Sunday school, for Chrissake!"

"The guy told me the truth about my life, Patrick. No drug or mushroom or even a woman has ever done that for me. I can't explain it to you, but...look, we're thirty years old, we've read about some pretty wild shit that's happened to other people and it sounded really far out, and wouldn't it be great if we could meet a sorcerer or some kind of master, and we could trip out on the magic. It was really great to think about it and talk about it, but..." He paused to search for the right words and, in spite of myself, I was impressed by the intensity of his expression. If it hadn't been Peter, I would have sworn it was a look of sincerity. "...but it never happened for us, Pat. And now I'm not even sure that it happened for those guys in the books. And even if it did—so what? All I know is that all the time we talked about that stuff and wished it could happen for us, my life was bleeding away on me. It's just like

I said about sex, I think about it all the time, but…it's all mostly thinking. And meanwhile life is happening and I'm not even here for it. So maybe this guy Xavier isn't Don Juan or Rolling Thunder. And maybe it'll be boring as hell. But to tell you the truth, man, my life is already boring as hell. That's why I spend so much of it trying to be somewhere else."

"Mr. Party finally comes clean," I said in wonder.

"Not really," he explained, "I ain't planning on giving up the booze or the drugs or the women until I get a better offer. But I am going to give this guy my best shot."

"Yeah, but what about the money?" I demanded. "Sixteen G's is a lot of cash."

"I've pissed more than that away at the tracks—or buying drinks for women who didn't come home with me later," Peter replied philosophically. "It's like he said: how much have we ever really given to ourselves? And what the hell are we making money for if we don't enjoy any of it?"

"I don't know," I objected stubbornly, "I just don't think it's right to be charging people for this kind of thing. It's not…spiritual. And there's no guarantee that we're going to enjoy it, or even get anything out of it."

"Well, I can't explain this, but something inside me wants to go for it. I don't know if it's that voice he was talking about, or if I'm just fed up with what's happening in my life, but I get the feeling that I'm going to be seeing a lot of Mr. X over the next little while. You probably will, too."

"You know something I don't get, Peter? All the time I was going out to that shack, you were putting it down to complete lunacy. Now when it really does look insane to me, you become the great seeker. How come we keep switching like this? How come we never have the same point of view?

"Because yours is always wrong," he explained. "Just loosen that old Scottish grip on your money belt and admit that you want to see him again."

"I'm not so sure," I insisted. "It's not only the cost—it's the principle of the thing. Charging money for spiritual growth is…I dunno, it's…dirty or something."

"Yeah, well, add your principles to a five dollar bill," Peter suggested, "and you can afford to buy us the next round."

I walked home a little light-headed and a lot depressed. This was not an unusual state for me to be in, since depression was one of the few constants in my life, almost like an old friend who had latched on to me so long ago that I could hardly imagine life without him. But this time there was an added sense of loss, as though I had reached that place in the road where the next step seemed to be off a cliff. I was looking for something that would satisfy some need in me, but I was afraid to look at what the need was. Every time it reared its ugly head, my life went down the toilet. I would lose a relationship, flub an important opportunity, or just plain embarrass myself with its starkness and the foolish acts it would drive me to. Whenever I felt needy, I became capable of anything—from latching on to people until they forced me away, to being so obsequiously helpful that no one would have the heart to shun me. Sometimes, to get a woman to stay with me, I would all but lick her feet in admiration, and lie so blatantly about how much I loved her that the memory of it years later could still make me cringe with disgust. That was now all deep in my past, but it left me with the grim determination to never again feel its sickening power.

So here I was, caught between a rock and a hard place. If I returned to Xavier, he would probably expose me to aspects of myself that I couldn't bear to look at, much less let others see. But if I didn't return, I had only the dreary routine of coping to look forward to. Maybe I was just born that way, or perhaps my family played a part in it, but all my life I had felt driven to find something. Through all my travels and all my adventures, of which there were many (Peter made sure of that), there had always been something lacking. The lack would always lead me back to this gradually growing depression which was now my constant companion. Something inside told me that Xavier was my only option.

In the moment I thought of him, there seemed to appear before me a crack in my world. It wasn't so much visual as a 'felt-sense'. In that half-second I saw my physical reality split in two, and as the crack widened I caught a glimpse of what lay beyond that which I had always thought of as the 'real world'. The utter nothingness was terrifying; I felt myself both falling into it and away from it simultaneously. My head whirled and my heart pounded fiercely and I was certain that I was either dying or going insane. It was like a nightmare where all sense of control was lost and what remained was total helplessness, but just as quickly as it came, it stopped and the walls of my world slammed back shut, leaving no sign. I found myself standing in the middle of the street, holding my head and shaking.

Then I heard his voice. "*There is no place you can go where I will not come to be with you. Choose between this world to which you have made yourself a victim, and the real world that is your home.*"

But there was nothing beyond this world, I thought.

"*Nothing that you are ready to see,*" he responded. "*But what seems to be death or insanity to you now is what keeps you chained here. You didn't look with your heart. I'm giving you the choice: choose for your heart or for your smallness. On either path I'll be with you, but only on one can you be with me. Choose wisely now.*"

What was it you just did there?

"*You said you wanted Castaneda.*" He laughed, and I realized that I was standing two blocks from where I should have been. What amazed me the most was not the sight of my world falling away or the emptiness beyond, or even that words seemed to have been placed in my head. With the urging to choose came a wonderful feeling of compassion and deep caring, purely for me. With tears in my eyes, I recognized that I had done nothing to deserve it. Usually I had to do something to get even a scrap of affection, but I couldn't think of anything that could draw this kind of feeling to me. How could anyone love me that much? And why should they?

Soon a steady stream ran down my face, tears of gratitude mixed with an inexplicable sadness. I have no memory of the long walk home, yet I do know that everything I looked at was new and fresh, even the garbage that littered the streets looked entirely beautiful to me. "Alright," I spoke peacefully to the night sky, "I really don't have anything to lose anyway."

Working on my procrastination list was a lot harder than I thought it would be. I realized too late that Mr. X had never explained what we had missed, so when I looked at my list, I immediately started thinking about doing something else. I had until Saturday morning anyway, and it was getting late. Maybe I should even wait until I had talked to Xavier before I completed it. The more I thought about it, the more appealing became the idea to go to bed now, so I put the paper aside and headed for my room. When I flicked on the switch in the hallway, I was greeted by the accusing darkness. Determinedly, I marched into the kitchen and retrieved a bulb from one of the cupboards. Grabbing a chair along the way, I climbed up and changed the light. The glow that lit up the hall gave me a tiny boost—enough energy, at least, to return the chair rather than leave it in the hallway for a few days, which was my tendency.

When I entered the kitchen, a mound of precariously stacked unwashed dishes called to me from the sink: Patrick Kennedy—this is your life. I became aware of how tired I felt. Not from the time of night, but from the perception of how overwhelming my life seemed to me. I stared at the dishes, mentally reviewing my list of unfinished business: the items on the list were all just more work, giving me nothing. My days were so full of obligations and duties that when I came home I just wanted to relax, maybe sit in front of the tube for a few hours and veg out, or pop over to the pub for a couple of brew and a game of pool. Just thinking of having to pay some bills or return a few calls, or whatever, depleted me of the small amount of energy I had left. I could feel myself tiring noticeably by merely looking at the stack of dishes. And if, as Xavier had stated, this was just the tip of the iceberg, I shuddered to think what demands lay lurking beneath the surface, waiting to smother me with their weight.

With grim determination, I waded into the thick of the Battle of the Unwashed Dishes, until every last knife, fork, pot and pan was dried and put away. Afterwards I went to my desk and cleaned up my bills, placed the library books at the front door to remind me to take them back in the morning, and phoned in to my dentist's answering machine to book an appointment. Then I looked over my list of incompletes: I had hardly even put a dent in them, and the man had said that my list had only scratched the surface. Looking over my priority list only gave me a vague feeling of lethargy, but no clearer idea of what Xavier expected. Oh well, I would show up at his place on Saturday and plead ignorance. I shrugged and went to bed, pleasantly surprised by a sensation of lightness inside me, instead of the dreary weight that usually accompanied my slumber.

The last thing I thought of that night was a segment of a

story whose origin I couldn't remember.

He called to them, but they were afraid and they ran away. He called to them again but they hid themselves. He called to them again but they stayed hidden, shaking in their fear. He called to them again...and a few came forward...and he pushed them off the cliff...and they flew!

THE WARRIOR'S DISCIPLINE

"As I told you last Tuesday, the Warrior's Resolve makes you the priority in your life. It is your fixity of purpose. Without it, no problem can be solved, nor any truly beneficial goal reached. You must make your happiness number one."

We had been in class for about half an hour, and after settling up with the money, the teacher dove right in, immediately confronting us again with the issue of our tardiness. Working like a patient dentist on a particularly stubborn tooth, he finally drew it out of me that I was resisting putting out that kind of money without a guarantee. I had to admit that I didn't trust Mr. Garth Xavier all that much. "You'd better not," he advised me. "You might start trusting yourself next!" At that point, he brought up the issue of the Warrior's Resolve.

"But isn't that kind of self-centred?" I inquired. "There's been a lot of damage done by people who only look out for number one, and walk over others in the process. If we all just thought of ourselves, then the whole world would be dog-eat-dog everywhere you looked."

"Spoken like a true Pleaser, Pat," the teacher smiled. "What would happen if you thought about yourself first?"

"I dunno, I just don't think like that—I have to consider others all the time."

"And if you did just think about you?"

"I'd probably feel too guilty to do it for very long."

"That's right. You see, it's not that it's true for you to always consider others first; it's just that you'd feel too guilty not to. If you really made yourself the priority in your life, how would it affect you?"

"I dunno, I don't even know what that means."

"Well...use your intuition."

"I don't know how," I responded, not mentioning that where I grew up only women had intuition. Garth continued patiently.

"Well, take a wild guess. If you were the priority—if you were to do something completely for yourself—would you feel good or bad?"

"Good, I guess, but only if no one got hurt by it?"

"But if it was something that truly made you happy, would that be a good thing for the world?"

"But hey, a lot of guys aren't like Patrick, Garth. A lot of them are only happy when they're walking on other people's faces to get what they want."

"Those people are neither happy, nor are they priorities in their own lives. Their priority is some kind of revenge on the world, and they're fighting a war they can't win."

"You wouldn't know it by the money and power they have."

"But how could they enjoy what was gained by someone else's loss?"

"Because they have no conscience, or any ethics, or morals," I stated.

"If you mean they aren't affected the way you are, the difference is only in how they react to their guilt. They may be in such deep denial of their feelings that they aren't aware of how that guilt is working on them." He walked up to the easel and drew what looked like a large test tube with horizontal lines crossing its length.

"Let's say this is your subconscious mind," he suggested.

"Looks like a ribbed condom," Peter remarked.

"Yes, one of my other students calls it the Prophylactic of Doom." Garth chuckled. "The subconscious mind is an appendage of the conscious mind. It's like a huge storage room filled with all the unfinished business in your life. It contains all your dysfunctional family dynamics, your sexual guilt, and tons of aggression."

"What about normal guilt?"

"That's a contradiction in terms," the teacher answered wryly, "but yes, that's there too—it's a big part of your family dynamics. The point is that human beings, discounting a very few, all have this appendage here. And it's loaded with bad feelings! This little sucker," he tapped his finger on the sketch, "can cause accidents, divorce, suicide, and keep you in a general state of misery for your whole life. The subconscious can even topple world governments. Those amoral people you mentioned have this inside them to the same extent that you do."

"What does the subconscious do though?" Peter asked. "I mean, what's its function?"

"For one thing, it keeps you from receiving what you want in your life, urging you to chase something on the one hand, while pushing it from you on the other. It keeps you constantly in a state of unworthiness, not letting you see that your own feelings and attitudes are keeping you from your goals. And then it encourages you to blame someone or something outside yourself for not being able to reach those goals. Ah yes, the subconscious mind—no victim should leave home without it!"

"Those people you mentioned, who walk over others— they might have hardened themselves against feeling bad about their actions, but no one can feel truly good inside if someone else suffers from their acts—whether they are aware of it or not."

"And in order for you to be a priority in your life, everyone has to benefit from the achievement of your goals and your purpose. How could you ever truly feel that you'd won anything if you had to bear the guilt of someone else's loss— how full would your victory be, and who would be there with you to celebrate it?"

"But people do it every day, Garth!" Peter insisted. "I know, because I'm one of them. And sure, I feel a little bad if someone gets hurt by what I do, but that's the way the rules are set up—and the guilt hasn't stopped me yet."

"It's true," I assured the teacher, "Peter's been a prick his whole life."

"Thank you, Pat," my friend said sarcastically. "And there are guys out there who are plenty worse than me."

"And you thought you got stoned and drunk because you liked it," Garth said with a mischievous glint in his eyes. Then he became serious again. "Look, it's simple: we can't be true to ourselves and choose an approach which does not benefit everyone because, on a deeper level, we're all joined to each other. The subconscious mind holds a record of every time we chose not to see that connectedness, as well as the bad, traumatic feelings we incurred from that choice. These lines on the drawing represent layers of the subconscious; let's say there are about two thousand per person. To clear one layer might take years. Of course, we spend more time making these levels than we do clearing them."

"Two thousand layers—holy doo-doo!" Peter commented wonderingly. "How long would it take to clear the whole thing out—if I really worked at it?"

"At the average speed? Oh I'd say a good two hundred and fifty. Lifetimes, that is."

"Jesus, what's the point of even trying?"

"Well, there's always the Warrior's Discipline," the teacher suggested.

"I've always hated that word," I said, shuddering.

"It's been said that there are two basic approaches to enlightenment: the path of discipline and the path of Grace. The path of discipline requires a concerted effort of mind training and physical austerities to keep one focused internally and away from the outside world. It is physically, emotionally and mentally demanding."

"Sounds like my last marriage," Peter snorted.

"Then there's the path of Grace. Grace is the force that uplifts you, and carries you toward your purpose, without effort. All that is required of you is what I call the Warrior's Discipline; it's the willingness and determination to *let* the grace carry you."

"I'll take door number two," Peter declared. I nodded my agreement.

"I thought you would," Garth smiled. "Which means you don't make drastic changes in your present lifestyle, but you do bring more awareness to your thoughts and actions, and simply be willing to let go of anything that is detrimental to your happiness. The Grace will do the rest. The Warrior's Discipline is the practice of 'effortless effort'."

"Sounds simple," Peter commented. "Maybe too simple."

"Yeah," I agreed. "If it was that easy, why didn't we do it a long time ago?"

"Why don't we find out? Tell me, Pat, what parts of your life aren't working for you?"

"Pick one," Peter chuckled.

"I can't think of one specific area at the moment."

"Well, for example, where are you not receiving in your work?"

"I'm sorry," I replied sincerely, "I really don't know what you mean. My work is going along fine. There are some things that I would have liked to see happen, but the cards didn't fall that way—not yet anyway."

"Like what?"

"Well, like two years ago, there was an opening to work with this psychologist in town who is really well-known. She was offering a chance for partnership, and it would have meant pretty good money—you know, more clients, and all my books and administrative stuff would have been handled by her people. It was a really great opportunity, and I was sure that I was the most qualified person around for the job, but I didn't get it. Actually, what happened was I completely blew the interview with her. I don't know how it happened, but she somehow got the idea that I was calling her a money-grubbing bitch, and that was that."

"Where did she get that idea?"

"Because he did call her a money-grubbing bitch," Peter informed him.

"It just slipped out," I explained pleadingly. "I didn't use that exact term—not at first—but when things started to get heated, my mouth took over and went off in a direction of it's own. It wasn't my fault. Anyway, I didn't get the job."

"And what else?" Xavier leaned forward, resting his chin in his hands and smiling mischievously.

"What, about my work? Well, there isn't much else," I

insisted. Then something occurred to me. "Oh! Well, there were a couple of times when my clientele was building itself up and then something weird would happen. Three times to be exact—but they were all beyond my control. I didn't do any of them."

"What happened?" the teacher urged.

"Well, one time there was a flu going around that kept me out of it for a month. By the time I got back on my feet, most of my clients had found someone else. The second time, I was really beginning to roll and I could just see the light at the end of the debt tunnel when this city decided to have its own little recession. A lot of companies just up and left, or closed down; coincidentally, they were mainly the companies that employed about half of my clients. And this last time I was nearly wiped out of work. I was just starting to get it together again, when my ex blind-sided me with divorce proceedings. Not only did the legal fees get me, but I spent so much time trying to work things out that I let my clients slip away."

"Well, I have to give you full marks for creative genius, Patrick," the teacher commended me. "You have had to pull some pretty novel stunts to make sure you don't move forward in your life."

"What d'you mean—I didn't do it on purpose. It was all way beyond my control—I had nothing to do with it," I insisted, then for good measure blurted out "I was a victim of the whole thing every time."

"That's what I mean, Pat—the way you set it up no one would ever be able to find your fingerprints on the detonator. You're such a good saboteur—and so cute!"

"One of these days I'm going to understand what the hell you're talking about," my friend declared. "How do you connect what happened with it being Kennedy's own doing? I mean, except for that interview, which he screwed up royally, all those other things just happened. Let's face it: shit happens!"

"Not to a Warrior," the teacher stated. "A Warrior is responsible for everything that happens in his life. To a Warrior, results equal intentions." He rose and went to the easel, printing in large letters,

RESULTS = INTENTIONS.

"Let's just look at it from a Warrior's point of view. What would have happened, Patrick, if you had landed that job with the psychologist?"

"I would have made more money," I replied. "And I would have had more free time."

"And what else?"

"I dunno...nothing, I guess." I thought about it for awhile. "I would have had more clients."

"Okay, now what would have been the results if things had not gone wrong all those other times?"

"I dunno... who can say how things would have turned out?"

"Well, take an intuitive leap. You know," he encouraged me, "use your intuition."

"I'm telling you, Garth, I don't have any intuition," I insisted apologetically.

"Sure you do—just, you know...take a guess."

"A guess? Okay," I sighed heavily, "my guess is that the same thing would have happened: more money, more free time—because I could hire extra help—and more clients."

"Okay, now let's just say that you didn't want any of these things to happen...why do you think that would be?"

"But I did want them! Why wouldn't I?"

"Funny, I thought I just asked you that."

"But I did want them," I insisted, suddenly feeling unaccountably irritated.

"Okay," he humoured me, "But let's just say that you didn't—you know, just for the heck of it. C'mon, indulge an old man. Let's just say that you didn't want more clients—just off the top of your head—why would that be?"

"I dunno. Maybe because..." I scratched my head, "it would be more of a drain?"

"And why would it be such a drain?"

"C'mon, Garth, counselling people who have problems takes a lot out of you."

"No," he corrected me, "it takes a lot out of you. So now you know why you sabotaged yourself. But let's keep going with this: you just give me the first answer that pops into your head, okay? Now, why don't you want more free time?"

"I dunno," I shrugged, "That was the first thing that

popped into my head."

"Okay, and if you did know why you didn't want more free time, what would your answer be?"

"I don't know. Because I wouldn't know what to do with it, maybe?"

"Good answer! Now what about money—why don't you want more money in your life?"

"Because he's crazy," Pete opined.

"Maybe. But why else?"

"But I do want money! D'you think I like being in debt all the time?"

"You don't have to like it to want it, Patrick. But just play along with me, just a little bit more. Finish the sentence: I like debt more than having money because…"

"It's safer," I blurted. "But that doesn't—"

"And," the teacher continued over my voice, "it's safer because…"

"I don't know; it doesn't make—"

"And if I did know why it was safer, I'd say it's because…"

"Because money is too much responsibility," I stated. "I don't get it—this doesn't make sense."

"It doesn't have to," Garth assured me. "And if I knew when money became such a big responsibility to me, I'd have to say it was around the age of…"

"Twenty-six. When my daughter Maya was born."

"That's probably when you started to really feel its effects, but let's just say that it started way back in your past. That you decided money was too big a responsibility for you. When would that have been?"

"I don't know, Garth. Really, I hardly remember anything about my childhood."

"Most people can't, especially around the times when they made their most destructive decisions. That's why you're better off going with your intuition."

"But I don't have any intuition."

"Everyone has intuition—it's a purer form of thought. We just don't access it because it's not as readily obvious as our intellectual processes. But let's just pretend that you have an intuition, even if you don't believe men are supposed to have such a thing—not real men, anyway. Now, if you were to know when you decided that money was just a big burden, it was probably around the age of...?"

"The number three popped up, but I feel like I just made that up."

"That's okay, that's okay.... Now if you were to know who you were with at the time, it was probably...?"

"Well, first I see my father, then my mother."

"And if you were to know if it was your mother or father, you'd probably say it was...?"

"Both is the answer that just popped up, but—"

"How long is this going to go on for?" Peter interrupted.

"That depends on Patrick," the teacher responded.

"Well then, move your ass there, P.K. I'm getting bored."

"If you're bored, Peter, it's because you're sitting on something, either your excitement or your support for Patrick. Boredom is a signal that something transformative can happen, but that you'd rather stay where you are. That goes for your whole life—not just in this room."

"So what do you want me to do? Be his cheerleader or something?"

"It's the most powerful kind of leadership in the world. On second thought, maybe you'd better just stay bored. We wouldn't want anything new or exciting to happen here," Garth suggested good-naturedly.

"Okay, okay, I get your point." Cairn smiled, and the teacher turned back to me.

"Now, Pat, what was going on between your Mom and Dad at the time—it was probably something like...?"

"Nothing. I see this picture of the three of us in the living room, but they're not talking to each other and I'm just playing with my blocks."

"And if you were to know why they weren't talking to each other, it was probably because...?"

"Aw, gimme a break!" I objected. "How the hell am I supposed to know what they were thinking?"

"Trust me," the teacher insisted. "What's the first thing that pops up? The reason they weren't talking to each other was...?"

"Because they didn't know how," I finished, feeling a sudden surge of anger. "Because they were mad at each other."

"And they were mad at each other about...?"

"I dunno...about sex. And money."

"And the concern about these was...?"

"Dad wanted sex and Mom was mad because she was pregnant and we were having money problems. But hey, look Garth, I feel like I just made this whole thing up! It's not like I really remember all this stuff."

"Just trust the process, Patrick. I'll explain later. So what have we got so far?"

"We're in the living room and they're having a fight about sex and money. She's not putting out for him and..." I trailed off weakly.

"What's the matter?"

"Nothing. I just realized that I never thought of my parents as having sex, and I never talked about her that way. Y'know, when I said 'putting out'. Like it was some kind of business deal or something."

"Is that the way your father felt?"

"I dunno...I guess so." Instinctively, I closed my eyes, and saw a picture of myself playing at my mother's feet, while both my parents sat across from each other, their noses stuck in some reading material.

"Okay, now Patrick," the teacher urged me quietly, "go back to that time and see yourself in that situation."

"I'm already there," I informed him, "but the picture keeps fading and shifting."

"Okay, don't worry about it; just let it stay as much as it wants. Now, what are you feeling?"

"I'm feeling okay."

"No, in that scene, what are you feeling?"

"Okay." I shrugged, "I seem to be pretty happy, but I'm kind of nervous and I keep wanting them to talk to me or to each other."

"And your father is feeling...?"

"Heavy. I think he's feeling like a failure."

"And the reason he feels like that is because...?"

"Because Mom doesn't like him. Or respect him, but she's not really saying that—it's just a feeling. And that's even worse—that she's not saying it." I let my thoughts go where they would, watching the scene shift slightly but not really change all that much. "Now I'm beginning to pick up more from Dad. It's like he feels that she won't love him because he doesn't make enough money—"

"Just like a woman," Peter sniffed derisively.

"Patience, Mr. Cairn," Xavier advised him, "We'll get into your knickers later. So what's happening now, Patrick?"

"Well, I think I need your help here, Garth. My mind is going all over the place."

"It usually does when you start getting close. So your mother won't love your father unless he makes more money, and the reason your father doesn't want to do that is because…?"

"Because he hates his job. He's a plumber. So he feels like her love's not worth it, if he has to work even harder to get it. He's deciding that he'll just do without love. I don't know where these ideas are coming from, but that's what I get."

"Great, just trust it. So now what decision do you, as a three year old, make about money?"

"That it sucks."

"And what else?"

"That it causes separation between people. That if it weren't for money, people would love each other more."

"So what do you decide to do about money?"

"To keep it away from me."

"Good, now let's go a little deeper. What is your father feeling toward your mother because she won't give him sex?"

"He's pissed at her. He feels like it's his right as her husband, but she keeps telling him that she doesn't feel good because she's pregnant, or she's too tired, or something to that effect."

"And what's he feeling under the anger?"

"Well, it feels like…" I became puzzled. "Like he's hurt. He seems to be crying inside. He feels that he's done his best for us, but that he's failed us somehow and he doesn't deserve to be loved. I know this sounds strange, but I keep getting the hit that he thinks his wife hates him, and that if she screwed him he would be forgiven. Shit, this can't be for real, man! I never saw my old man hurt in my whole life."

"You'd be surprised at what children can see. And feel."

"And it seems that my mother feels like she failed, even though it looks like she's making it his fault."

"So he's blaming her and she's blaming him, but beneath all that, they both feel like they've failed the other. And at that point, what are you feeling about the whole situation?"

"I was just thinking about that," I replied. "I get the idea that somehow I felt like it was all my fault. I don't know why, but when I get a picture of myself back then, it looks like I think I'm the reason there's no money, and that I'm the reason everybody's so unhappy, but I can't figure out what it was that I did to cause it all. I even feel that I'm the reason they're not having sex."

"So what decision do you make about yourself at this time?"

"I dunno...I guess I decide that I'm a failure; that I could've done something and I didn't."

"And what do you decide about life?"

"That it's too much trouble; you work hard and do your best to get ahead, but all it means is that you fall on your face farther up the road. I've felt like that a lot." This last realization was accompanied by a wave of self pity.

"So," the teacher inquired in a quiet tone, "trying to improve the quality of your life just means more hard work, more sacrifice, is that it?"

"Something like that, I guess."

"Well, at least we know why you've been effectively sabotaging your work situation."

"We do?" Pete grunted, "I don't get it."

"Me neither," I agreed, "How could some decision I made when I was three years old be affecting me now?"

"Because that same decision is being played over in your subconscious every day. Time is different in there."

"So how can it make things happen in the world—all that sabotage you say I've been doing to my work?"

"Easy. You look at money as something that keeps you away from love, you look at your work as a burden, and you look at free time as just a chance to feel more bored and frustrated with your life. Those were pretty much your words, weren't they? To you, success is a big burden—a sacrifice, so why cross another bridge? Just kaboom! Blow the sucker up!"

"But how can having money be a sacrifice to me? I know it's not!"

"In your conscious mind, yes. Consciously you look at money as something that will give you a great amount of relief, if not happiness. But unbeknownst to you there is a three-year-old child who holds a stronger conviction. One that says money is the cause of all separation, and hatred, and pain in this world. From the results of your present situation, which belief is being more closely adhered to? Your present financial situation is designed to keep money away from you—and where do you think that design originated? From that three-year-old's choice."

"But that's…that's not fair!" I stammered.

"Are you ready for more?" the teacher ignored my last remark. "Look inside and see the little child again in that situation you described before. He's feeling guilty because he thinks that what's happening is somehow his fault. Have you got it?"

"Yeah, kind of," I answered, my eyes closed.

"How is the child feeling?"

"Terrible—like he's being crushed or something."

"Okay. And how do you feel watching him in that picture?"

"The same. Maybe not as strongly as the little me, but I sort of feel that crushing in my chest."

"So what do you decide about yourself, then?"

"I dunno…I guess I think there's something wrong with me. Something bad."

"So what do you decide to do about it?"

"Become good?" I guessed, "I don't know—you tell me."

"Just guess," Xavier encouraged me, "and trust your hunches."

"Okay, I guess I decided that I somehow caused hurt to people, and that I'd do my best to make it better. Somehow."

"How?"

"By being good. And by helping them when I see they're hurting."

"So you think you caused the pain, and now you're going around bandaging the wounds?"

"Yeah…something like that."

"Sounds like a counsellor to me," Garth stated.

"You mean I decided to become a counsellor when I was three? I didn't even know what a counsellor or a psychiatrist was."

"Well, the details came to you as your need to pay off your guilt developed. The helping profession is full of people trying to pay off childhood debts. The trouble is the guilt hardly gets touched by the helping acts, so pretty soon the job becomes a big sacrifice: all work and no reward. I don't blame you for not wanting more clients, Patrick. It would probably kill you."

"So let me get this straight," Peter interrupted. "Pat here is closing down companies, giving himself the flu, and divorcing his wife—all on purpose? I've got a good imagination, Garth, but I'd have to stretch it into another dimension to believe this one."

"I told you he was creative." Garth winked at me conspiratorially. "So now what we have looks something like this: we have a man who is working to pay off his guilt. Since it is a self-induced punishment, he can't really let himself enjoy it. Also, he sees money as a bad thing, so he can't let himself have that; what he can't keep away from himself, he uses to pay off more debts, or to help other people, like his wife and daughter. He keeps nothing for himself except the bare necessities, and even such luxuries as vacations are only taken to give him enough strength to perpetuate his state of sacrifice."

"Damn, Pat, how's that for an autobiography?" Peter asked, amazed. I was too stunned to reply. I wanted to say something in my defense, but the only words that came to me were, it's not my fault!

"Now," the teacher continued, "that scene, or one very much like it, is being played repeatedly in your subconscious basement, and you're making decisions for your happiness based on the mistaken beliefs of a hurt, confused three-year-old. It all happened as a result of choosing to feel that you had failed, Patrick."

"Wait a minute, he didn't choose that!" Peter objected, voicing my sentiments. "He found himself in a screwed-up situation that made him feel like that. He was only three, for Chrissake. It was the situation that made him feel like he failed."

"Did it? Or did his interpretation of the situation influence how he felt? For now, let's play it my way—my rules, okay? Good. Now Patrick, are you still feeling terrible?"

"Worse, now that you've convinced me that it was all my fault."

"You didn't need any help with that. So, first you said your parents were silently blaming each other, then you said that beneath the blame, they both were feeling hurt."

"Yeah, and I feel like I should do something—that it's my fault that they're hurting." I was surprised to feel tears welling up in my eyes, but Peter's presence helped me force them back.

"Okay, just stay with the feeling," the teacher reminded me. "Now, how do you feel towards your parents—as the three-year-old?"

"Cut off. I feel like we're all in little shells, screaming to get out." My chest began to ache.

"Good. Now why don't you ask for help?"

"Help?" I said, as if it were a foreign word. "From whom?"

"I don't know—but don't you feel the need to? Yes? Just follow that impulse, and call out to whatever power is greater than you and the scene in your mind. Give it a shot and see what happens." I focused my attention on the child and felt something reaching out of me, a kind of pleading or beseeching. After a short time, I thought I could see a beam of light penetrating the top of the child's head from above.

"How does that feel?"

"It feels okay," I shrugged, actually feeling a little better.

"And how do your parents look?"

"About the same—they've still got their noses in their books," I said. "Actually, I can see that they're hurting a lot more easily, now."

"So can you hear their calls for help?"

"Not really—what do you mean?"

"Don't you realize that you're seeing the pain beneath their anger, and that their pain is actually a call for help? If you see somebody hurting, they're really just calling out for love. Now, why don't you respond to that call? See yourself giving love to your mother."

"How?" I asked, feeling uncomfortable with the word love being used so freely.

"In whatever way feels best; whichever way the light directs you. Just trust the process."

"Okay," I assented, my eyes still shut as I viewed the inner scene, "I see myself getting up and giving her a hug."

"And how does she respond?"

"She's pushing me away," I told him, feeling rejected.

"That's probably because you want something from her; you want her to get better, or to play with you or something. Why don't you just give her some nice affection; she can remain unhappy if she wants, and you can love her like that— for no particular reason. Just because you love her. Try that."

And so I did, surprised at how difficult it was to even conceive of at first, because it occurred to me that I did want something from her. It was the same sensation I'd had around my wife in the last year of our marriage. What I desired was not quite clear to me, but I had been nagged by it day and night. And the more it had compelled me, the more irritated Darlene had become. My sexual desire grew and hers lessened; my need to spend more time with her coincided with her becoming more busy at work. And damn if it didn't happen that every time I wanted to talk about our relation-ship, one of her friends would phone for a marathon conversation. Sometimes I would follow her around the house, or phone her many times a day to talk to her about things of little consequence, until finally, one day, she turned on me, screaming, "What do you want from me? Go get a life of your own, for Chrissake!"

At that point, I turned and walked out of the house, returning only to collect my belongings and say good-bye to Maya. Since then, I had been afraid that the tortuous feeling of raw, unidentifiable need would return, and destroy some other part of my world. And here it was, in both me and the three-year-old who used to be me, coursing through my veins like poison.

I saw myself approaching my mother again, and again she pushed me back. I didn't want Peter or Xavier to know what was happening, so embarrassed was I by the surging, unbridled need that threatened to possess me.

"Don't block your emotions," Garth said soothingly, as if he knew what was happening. "Just be aware of what you're feeling, don't wrestle with it."

"She's rejecting me," I pouted in spite of myself, then added, "as usual."

"Only because you're still trying to take something from her." It was true; I could feel my neediness clawing at her.

"But she's the grown-up here; she's supposed to be giving

to me!"

"You're so busy trying to get something from her, that you don't even recognize her anymore. Can't you see she feels that she has nothing to offer you? She has failed as a wife and a mother in her eyes."

"But she was a great mother!" I blurted tearfully.

"Then let her know that. She's losing her sense of worth, and you're demanding something of her that only makes her more aware of what she thinks she lacks. Don't try to take from her, Patrick—give. Show her that she's worth loving."

"I'm trying!" I pleaded, "but that kid just feels too needy. I hate him for that—I hate me for that. That's what screwed up my family. And my marriage."

"Only because you looked to the wrong place to have your needs met. Why not let the light take care of your needs?"

"Because I'm ashamed of them," I hissed vehemently.

"Welcome to the human race," Garth said, but I was not in the mood for humour.

"I hate how weak it makes me feel!" I wanted to reach inside and wring the three-year-old's neck; to throw him out the window or smash his head to a pulp. "You've ruined everything, you little bastard! My marriage, my childhood…my whole goddamn life!" I pounded the arms of the chair in frustrated rage. "God, I hate life…I hate you!"

"Okay, feel all of that, Patrick, but there's no need to hurt yourself. Keep moving through it—don't get caught up in it. And keep asking for help." Keep asking for help? I hadn't even considered that.

"Help me," I pleaded.

"I'm right there with you. Just keep asking for the light, and trust it. Want to give love to your mother, just want to." As wave after wave of self-loathing broke over me, I pleaded inwardly for…something. At first there was no change, but gradually I saw the three-year-old me move once more toward my mother, and touch her gently on the knee. She moved my hand away, and in spite of the hurt that welled up in me, I climbed up and sat beside her, gently stroking her hair. She broke into an effluvium of tears, but my little hand kept moving through her locks as she cradled her head and shook with the sobs. Soon, my father was beside me, reaching over to comfort her and, wonder of wonders, there were a few tears threatening to run down his cheeks as well. Inside me, I realized that for years I had been longing to see my parents hold each other.

I don't know how I ended up on my knees on the floor, or for how long I cried while both Peter and Garth hugged and soothed me in reassuring tones. In my chest a sweet pain throbbed, and I was aware of a long-forgotten sensation: I felt alive. A tissue materialized before me and I took it to wipe my eyes, then another to blow my nose. A few minutes and several tissues later, we returned to our seats. I was feeling familiarly self-conscious, and unable to meet the eyes of either Peter or Garth. A long silence followed until, after shifting about in my seat, I glanced sheepishly at both of them and mumbled a shy thank you.

"You're welcome," Xavier replied.

"Any time!" Peter added cheerfully.

"But we're not finished yet," the teacher informed me, "Go back to that scene in your head and tell us what you see."

"I see all three of us down on the floor, playing with my blocks."

"And what do you decide about money now?"

"That it's…" I started, but then paused to consider the question, "…no big deal."

"And what does that mean?" Xavier wondered.

"Well, I'm not sure how to say this, but it's like…it's nothing, it's not some horrible thing that can ruin lives. As long as there's love, nothing matters; and if there's no love, then…nothing matters."

"So it's okay to have money?" Xavier asked.

"Yeah," I shrugged lightly. "It's fine."

"Good, that's a good start," Garth commended me.

"I still don't get it," Peter shook his head, "how does fooling around in your imagination help you—it doesn't change what really happened. Not that what you did wasn't great, but…what good did it really do?"

"Why don't we ask Patrick?" Garth suggested, looking into my eyes, "How do you feel now when you think of your mother and father?"

"Fine," I replied, thinking of their faces, "I never realized how much it meant to me to see them happy. It feels…great!"

"Okay, so now when he thinks of his old man, he's going

to have a good feeling inside," Peter persisted doggedly. "But what real good does it do him? Out there in the world today ?"

"Well, first of all, any time you take a bad or painful situation from the past, and let it be transformed into love in the present moment, you have allowed a miracle to come into your life. At this moment, Patrick feels better about himself— and his parents—and he's let a little more love in. That in itself is enough. As far as what good it'll do him, we'll just have to wait and see. But any time you clear away a destructive program in the subconscious, some area of your life will improve. Remember what I said about you being causal: your feelings directly determine the condition of your 'real world'. If you clear away a level of guilt and pain in your subconscious, then your whole life moves ahead one giant step. Once that happens, something else will come up to block you, or at least try to block you, but…one thing at a time. After all, what else is time good for?" As the teacher spoke, I continued to float on the waters of my new-found tranquility, my mind unusually quiet, and my chest feeling warm and expanded. I felt like I had already had my two-thousand-bucks worth. The grandfather clock in the hallway sounded the twelve o'clock chimes—and brought a tear to my eye.

"That was just a small sample of the Warrior's Discipline; by himself, Patrick could do nothing to change his beliefs or the way he saw his parents, and it could have taken him years to find that block, let alone get over the guilt and pain. But with his willingness to see the past differently and his determination to let the healing process happen, well…the light took care of the rest—almost instantaneously. Now," the teacher announced, "I have some homework for you."

"What—are we finished for the day already?" Peter demanded.

"No, I want you to start working on this assignment over lunch. You can return as soon as you complete it. And another thing, this course goes on twenty-four hours a day; awake or asleep. Whatever happens to you until this course is complete, it's all part of your Warrior's training. There are no accidents, or coincidences—they are all part and parcel of your training. After all," he winked at me, "I want to make sure you get your money's worth."

"Okay—so what's the assignment?"

"I want you both to go out and," he paused to look at each of us evenly, his eyes never losing that glint of harmless mischievousness, "receive your next partnership." Peter and I exchanged puzzled glances, and then turned to share them with Garth.

"What d'you mean?" I inquired. "What are we supposed to do?"

"You're not supposed to do anything. Just go out and leave yourselves open to the mate who's been waiting to come into your life. A Warrior's whole life is not about doing anything. It's about receiving; it's about letting. The most important words in the English dictionary are 'to let'."

"Just like that?" Peter asked with a hint of sarcasm. "I don't know how it is for you, Garth, but I'm out there every single night—and day—and either I'm blind, or there's a marked lack of available women."

"It's true," I agreed, "every single woman in this city is either attached, gay, or hates men. We've looked, believe me."

"You've looked through the eyes of someone who wants to take something. Your assignment is to go out and receive. Remember the Warrior's Discipline—effortless effort. Be willing to have a relationship in your life, and be determined to let it come to you."

"We have been," Peter insisted, "at least I have! And except for the occasional short-termers and one-nighters, no one has shown up for me to receive. I tell you, I work at it every night, giving the woman who's right for me every chance to meet me."

"That's the problem, Peter, you're working too hard for it."

"But that's me—that's the way I am."

"Yes, and look at the results; no partnership for how long?"

"About two, maybe three years—not including the short-term ones. You know, for a week or two."

"Three years—and you, Patrick?"

"Well, I'm still getting over my divorce," I explained weakly.

"A Warrior never uses excuses. Neither of you have had a partnership with a woman in a long time. You spend most of your days thinking about it, but you won't let yourselves have one, mainly because you look at everything to do with them as just so much work."

"They are work!" Pete exclaimed.

"Only because of your unwillingness to receive. I know this may sound completely insane to you, but work is an insult to all that is true in life. What you call work is really a refusal to allow yourselves to be given to. And the entire universe is at your disposal, waiting to serve you. Look at nature. But don't just look at it; look into it, and you'll see what makes it so beautiful. It's in a state of total surrender, total acceptance of the energy that allows it to exist. But you! You think you have to earn everything that you get in life—you don't realize that even the concept of earning came from a decision that you were not worthy simply to receive."

"If you were to question the habits and patterns that occupy your time, I'm sure you'd come up with logical, rational explanations for all of them. I know how much you value those intellects of yours, but have you ever noticed that those habits and patterns are not aimed at your happiness? They may be aimed at maintenance, or even survival, but survival for what? Do you want to survive just so you can go on living in your habits and patterns—surviving to survive?"

"What was it I said that set you off?" Peter asked, but Garth ploughed through.

"Did you ever think that maybe the reason you're not completely happy with your lives is because the habits and patterns of your day-to-day existence leave no room for happiness? And did you ever think that maybe the reason for holding on to those habits was to keep the happiness out? Purposely?"

"That's stupid," I commented.

"Yes, but since when has that stopped you?"

"And a relationship is going to change all that—assuming that what you say is true?"

"You know in your heart whether it's true or not, Patrick. No, the relationship won't give you that, but it will show more clearly where you're not willing to receive in your life, where you feel too unworthy to receive. Did you finish your list of incompletes?" We both admitted our negligence, but Xavier continued, unaffected. "Well, your next intimate relationship will embody that list, believe me. It will bring up all the issues in your life to be resolved or let go of, most of the time in ways you won't appreciate, at least not at first."

"This assignment isn't about achieving something, at least not in the way you think of it. It's about the Warrior's Discipline: a Warrior recognizes that life is a gift—it can in no way be bought or earned, and so everything on the Warrior's path is there to teach receiving. A Warrior resists nothing and desires nothing, but simply accepts what is. And everything that lies ahead takes the Warrior to the next level of awareness, if it's simply received. Now—"

"But," I couldn't remain silent any longer, "to be honest with you Garth, when I think of going into another relationship, it just looks like more shit and abuse to me. Except for the sex and occasional times when we're both in a good mood, most of it is painful, boring, or just one big hassle after another. That's been my experience; why should it be any different the next time out?"

"Yeah," Peter added, "and then you throw a kid or two in on top of that, and you don't even have a life of your own anymore. What's the bloody point? What the hell are relationships for, anyhow?"

Garth smiled warmly at us both. "Well, at least now you know why you haven't met any available women. You've got a special radar system for them, and if you get within a mile of one, you'll rearrange your whole day to make sure you don't meet her. It's probably a subconscious habit you have that even you don't know about. But," he added coyly, "don't mind me. To answer your question, a relationship in itself will give you nothing. It will simply mirror your inner process, just as the world does all the time. The advantage of an intimate sexual relationship is that it will take you into deeply emotional areas, old heartbreaks, that are waiting to be healed. Some of these areas can be reached through our teacher-pupil relationships, but a sexual partnership accelerates the process. It will bring up your sexual wounds more quickly and intensely."

"Well, that certainly makes the whole idea more attractive," Peter said.

"What's so special about a partnership that it can speed things up like that? Why can't I just do it on my own?" I asked.

"Basically," the teacher explained, "one dynamic of the human psyche is that we entered our chosen family with the intention of serving them. Somewhere along the line we seem to have forgotten that, and that's where the separation problem began. Patrick, in the process we just completed, your problem with your mother began when you decided to try to take something from her rather than give to her. Only in giving can you truly receive anything."

"But I was only a little kid—what did I know?"

"Oh, quit whining dammit!" Peter snapped, and we all laughed.

"It was a mistake," Xavier explained. "It wasn't anybody's fault. You forgot, at that moment, that you had come to serve your parents; to love them unconditionally. As a result, a trauma, or fracture occurred which has affected you—your beliefs about money, sex, relationships…who knows what else, until this very day when you cleared it—with a little help from higher up. I don't suppose you've noticed that at least one or two relationships in your life have brought up this same trauma, have you?"

"Maybe," I conceded, wondering how he knew about Darlene. "But I made that whole thing up. That scene with me as a three-year-old with my parents—I didn't even get those playing blocks until I was five."

"Your imagination provided the setting, and it was probably more accurate than you think; but those feelings had been inside you for a long time. They've probably come up on a number of occasions—especially in your marriage. But since they happened without any understanding or conscious memory, they were probably treated as problems with the relationship. You probably thought that things went sour. Or that she changed, right?"

"Could be," I blushed, "I don't really remember."

"We men aren't known for our courage in the face of emotions," he laughed knowingly. "We'd rather fight off a couple of grizzlies than confront some deep feeling—and there's a ton of those feelings in the subconscious. A relationship helps confront them, and gives us the opportunity to let them be healed. We will be free of them eventually; it's my experience that a relationship can speed up the process."

"Oh boy!" Cairn announced, rubbing his hands together. "A chance to feel like shit—just what I've been looking for. And I thought all they had to offer was their bodies."

"You already feel like shit, Peter. But instead of trying to control your feelings with booze, or drugs, or..." he winked at my friend, "...masturbation, you can regain a part of yourself—a valuable part of yourself." He lifted himself out of his chair, signalling that it was time to go, but Peter wasn't finished.

"So you want us to go out and get a re–, sorry; I mean you want us to go out and receive a relationship, and then come back—right?"

"Right," Garth agreed.

"Okay, so let me see...forty-five, maybe fifty minutes for lunch...and what, another twenty for her to show up. So let's see...we ought to be back by two-ish." He looked me up and down a few times, then said, "Hmmm...better make that three-thirty to be on the safe side."

"It's not a matter of time," Garth informed us as we walked to the door, "it's a matter of willingness. Procrastinators always make time their boss. Just be willing, and let the universe take care of the rest."

We walked the eight blocks to our favorite restaurant, both reviewing the unusual events of the morning in silence. I noticed that my ribs and shoulders ached, probably from the emotional catharsis, and enjoyed the sensation.

"I dunno," my friend declared after we had taken our seats by the window, "At first I thought this was some kind of candy-ass trip, but after what he just said about relationships, I feel like it would be easier to jump off a cliff like Castaneda, or fight some demon, or something like that! The stuff he just talked about is...weird."

"I know what you mean," I agreed, "I wish it had something more solid to it...something I could sink my teeth into." I stopped to think about what I had just said, and then added, "Although, I do feel better after what happened. Whatever did happen."

"Well, all I know is that I just gave the guy a certified cheque for two thousand dollars so he could tell me to go find a woman. I could have given you the money to tell me that."

"Hell, yeah! And I would've only charged you half that much." We ate our meals and sat for a while, practising our version of the Warrior's Discipline: both willing and deter-mined to allow a woman to come into our lives, as long as she met certain 'liberal requirements'. Later we walked to a nearby park and sat on the benches beside a small duck pond, saying very little. We waited. Two hours of this brought us to the decision that it would be just as easy to 'let it happen' in some cozier atmosphere, with a beer in front of us, so we made our way over to the Elk's Horn.

"So, how are you doing?" Cairn inquired of me after the brew was delivered.

"The only female I've seen all day was that lady with the mustache in the café—and even she was taken," I answered. "Jeez, look around—there's not even a waitress in this place! What does he mean, 'be willing'? I think this whole thing is a crock." I began to suspect that Garth Xavier was some kind of smooth-talking con artist who had just relieved me of two thousand hard-earned dollars. "This whole world is one big rip-off!"

"And if you were to know when you first decided to believe that," Peter nudged me, "it was probably around the age of...?"

"Oh, screw off!" I laughed, nudging him back. I rose from my chair. "I'm going to the can; have two women here by the time I get back, okay?"

"I'll work on it," he assured me, then corrected himself, "I mean, I'll let it happen. But to tell you the truth, I feel more than a little foolish about this whole thing. If only my friends could see me now."

"What about me? I'm your friend."

"I mean my real friends; you know—the ones that matter."

Standing at the urinal, I stared at the graffiti I had read countless times in the past:

Do dyslexics worship a dog?

Kill the paranoids before they get us

If you love something, let it go. If it doesn't come back, chase it down and kill it!

There were also the offers of various sexual acts, and I realized, much to my surprise, that I could recite the words by memory—right down to the explicit details. I had been standing in that same stall reading those very same words and evacuating the very same beer for the last two years. My whole life was an endless loop of never-changing customs that I performed regularly with little conscious thought. And for what purpose—to what end? To keep me from feeling too much, I realized, as I moved away from the stall to wash my hands.

In the course of an average day, I would think a million thoughts, have maybe a dozen 'interesting' revelations about life, and say some profound words, but I couldn't recall a lot of powerful feelings coming through me with any regularity. Why had it been a surprise to me earlier to experience such strong love for my family? When I left home, my mother had held back her tears, my father had been drunk, and my four siblings had been away at a movie or something. Since then, I rarely thought of them, rarely even heard from them, and I wondered: if one of them died, would they call to let me know? Then I felt a shift inside me and I found myself caring about them. Their faces appeared in my mind as a flood of emotion washed through. Sometimes sad, sometimes angry, but most often simply concerned and caring. I even felt proud of them: Michael, who would give you the shirt off his back, and John, who could find humour in the midst of the most frightening or painful situation; Cathryn the beauty queen, who even had stray dogs and cats following her home—and wanted to keep every one of them, too. And of course Jaylene, the youngest as well as the smartest, who could floor you with the most embarrassingly astute observations about your behaviour. Such a fine collection of human beings—I wondered why I stayed away from them, why I never gave them much more than a passing thought.

A shadow passed behind me. A long shiver ran down my spine as I saw, reflected in the mirror, a tall thin man standing at the urinal, and I knew the answer. My father cast a very long shadow over our house. Even though he was actually quite short and plump, he made up for it with a very big temper. I don't remember when he started to drink, or much of what he was like before he did, but somewhere along the line I became painfully aware of the ever-growing shadow that slowly engulfed the entire family. It's hard to pinpoint what caused the most hurt; whether it was the unreasonable beatings, the endless volley of harsh criticism, or the uncertainty of what I would be coming home to each night—or how he would be when he came home. I guess the deepest hurt was looking at the fear and sorrow in the eyes of people I so deeply treasured. All their gifts, their love and their beauty seemed to have been lost as time went on and the shadow grew.

And then there was my mother, who, like most enablers, lived the life of a long-suffering saint. She never complained nor spoke ill of her husband, and probably never gave much time to the idea of leaving him, no matter how much the kids prayed for it to happen. It hurt to see her bear her yoke silently, but as time went by my compassion and understanding gave way to burning resentment and disrespect for her, as she stood by and watched him run amok with physical and psychological abuse. What kind of mother doesn't protect her young, I wondered disdainfully as I pulled away.

The bathroom was empty, and I figured that Peter would be having all kinds of warped thoughts about what I was doing in there, but I continued to look at my reflection.

I was afraid that if I involved myself in a relationship, I would become just like my father. No, that wasn't it. Not totally anyway.

I hated my mother, and took it out on all women. No, that was too easy. I felt into it a little deeper.

I was afraid that I was the shadow. That was it! I believed that I was just bad news looking for a place to happen; that I would bring only dreariness and hurt into a woman's life. I had put it on Dad because I didn't want to see it in me, but he was as much a victim to its curse as the rest of us. The shadow had appeared in all my romances and intimate relationships; not right away, but eventually, inevitably, I would bring ruination. Just ask Darlene. I felt that I was on the right track, but I needed to verify it with Garth. He would be able to help me break through the wall that kept healthy, loving relationships out of my life. I would bring it up with him right aw—

Oh-oh! I couldn't go back to him until I let the relationship in. But the shadow made that impossible. I was stuck for good, I decided with a sense of impending doom. Hoisted by my own petard!

> *I hope I'm wrong, because if I'm right...*
> *This is what I get!*

The graffiti was scrawled just to the right of the mirror. I was now feeling impressed by Garth's methods, convinced that he knew what I would have to face in order to actually take another run at the world of intimate relationships: something he had said about all our unfinished family issues resurfacing. I hadn't even seen a potential mate, and already the doo-doo was hitting the fan. I still wasn't sure that I wanted to go through with this particular means of healing my old wounds. Wasn't there some other path that I could take, one that didn't involve other people, one that I could walk alone? There had to be, I decided, because there was no way I was going to lay this on anyone else. I was tired of feeling like an ogre in some woman's eyes, tired of feeling like the mean Daddy to his daughter, tired of feeling that their lives had been better before I arrived, and would become that way again once I left. I was tired of feeling....

That's what it comes down to, P.K., I said to myself, you're tired of feeling. You're better off alone, without a woman, without any emotional hassle.... This way, at least, nobody gets hurt. Because sure as shit, if you get involved again, that's all that'll happen; people will be hurt.

> *I hope I'm wrong, because if I'm right...*
> *This is what I get!*

I don't know why, but suddenly the words made sense to me. I had been listening to the constant voice in my head for so long I just assumed that it told the truth. But what if it was wrong, and Garth was right? And how would I ever know who was telling the truth? How the hell does anybody make it through the maze of this life with any degree of confidence or guidance?

Listen to your heart, came the quiet response.

Okay, I thought to myself, I'm willing...to give this a try. I'm scared and I don't know how to just let something happen, and I have no idea what the hell Xavier is talking about most of the time, but (I exhaled heavily) I'm willing to have a relationship!

I was surprised with the difficulty I had over that word 'relationship', especially when it followed so closely the words, 'willing to have'. After all the days and nights I had spent looking for Ms. Right, only to end up alone and frustrated, I finally saw that underneath the frustration there had always been relief over my lack of success. I recalled something Xavier had said earlier that morning: "Warriors know that if they don't have something in their lives, it's because they don't really want it; they want something else more." Okay, I repeated more strongly, I'm—willing—to have a relationship in my life.

Peter and I had company. As I closed in on the table, I saw a woman on each side of my friend, both talking to him at the same time. His head swivelled back and forth, from one to the other, a rare smile of pure delight claiming his face. As I sat down, introductions were exchanged. Either I had been out of circulation for a long time, or Lisa and Jessica were two of the most lively souls I had ever met. They seemed to be full of fun, humour and sensitivity, with a real appreciation for life. To Lisa and Jessica, I must have seemed about as much fun as a foot fungus. The more they attempted to draw me out, the more I retreated into a near paralysis of speech and movement. I was caught in the dichotomy of trying 'to let', and feeling pressured to do something. My entire body was stiff with self-consciousness, and every time I was spoken to, I would mumble a response while rubbing an eye or scratching my nose, blocking my face from complete exposure. I was uncomfortably warm and fidgety, almost wishing the two women would leave, or that the ceiling would cave in on us— anything to end this misery! What, I kept asking myself, is the problem, Kennedy?

Then I remembered a remark of Garth's that had stuck in my mind: "A Warrior knows that he or she is greater than any feeling. Use your awareness. If what you are experiencing is

a true feeling, then your awareness will enhance it; if what
you're feeling isn't true, your direct awareness will shrink it,
leaving behind only what is true." Without closing my eyes,
I pulled my attention inward, letting myself sink into the shy,
awkward sensations that made me want to run and hide. My
body shook slightly, as though something else was in control.
The awkward, intense feelings increased every time Lisa or
Jessica looked at me, and damned if some part of me, usually
my face, would want to twitch! For Chrissake, Kennedy, get
a hold there—you're thirty-three years old! This isn't the
school sock hop! So this was what kept me away from women;
was I always like this? Had I felt this way when I met Darlene?

Yup, I recalled, only then I covered it over with fast-
talking. Now, for some reason, I didn't have the energy or
inclination to put that act on. I was more interested in what
lay underneath it.

The more I simply observed the feeling, the more I
realized how much of my life was governed by the threat of
its presence. Focusing on its very centre, I allowed it to engulf
me, and much to my surprise, it no longer had such a strong
control. My body relaxed more and stopped twitching. A
deeper sensation—of rejection, like a little boy sent to his
room, surrounded me. I was surprised to find that I was
feeling sorry for myself, but didn't let that stop me as I moved
my awareness into the centre of the rejection. There I found
another feeling, this one was of loneliness. In no more than
ten minutes I had experienced a collage of emotions and
sensations, each time going to their centres only to discover
something different as the previous one melted away. Finally,
I came to a place of calm and peace. As it grew, I lost my usual
inclination to drink myself to a "comfort zone." Good thing,
too—the intensity of my self-consciousness would have
demanded enough beer to fill my Pontiac's gas tank.

My first impression, as I looked over at Peter, was that he
was handling himself quite well, but then I noticed that he was
drinking a lot faster than usual. For Cairn, that meant the glass
was constantly in front of his face—which was probably his
plan. With my discomfort gone, I wanted to share my success
with him, encouraging him to give his awareness a chance,
but I did not want to advise him in front of our company. I
mouthed the words 'Warrior's Resolve' to him while Lisa and

Jess were conversing, but Peter could not lip-read too well. I attempted it a number of times, and then resorted to calling it out to him above the din of the bar. "I said use the Warrior's Resolve—just focus awareness on your feeling and be willing to let go of it—it's easy."

"What feeling—I'm not feeling anything," he replied, puzzled.

"Spoken like a true Independent!" Lisa announced, laughing.

"Oh no!" we both exclaimed, Peter and I looking at each other in disbelief. My friend turned toward the sandy-haired woman suspiciously, and demanded, "Did he send you here?"

"Who?" Jessica broke in.

"Garth—did he send you here to meet us?"

"What—you both know him too?" Lisa exclaimed. "How do you know about him?"

"Don't tell me you two guys are into that stuff too!" Jessica stated incredulously. "Garth Xavier? I thought he only wanted women groupies like Lisa here."

"We just started with him this week," Peter informed her. We then told the story of our encounters with the enigmatic Mr. Xavier. When we brought them up to the morning's lesson and our strange assignment, both women laughed.

"You mean," Jessica asked, "that you had to be told to go out and meet women? Isn't that some kind of basic drive in men?"

"That's not exactly what he told us," Peter explained, "he said for us to go out and receive our next relationship, and then come back. Isn't that what he told you, Lisa?"

"No, but I was already in one when I met Garth. As a matter of fact, it was right after my first class, when he told me the first principle—you know: 'Don't put off 'til tomorrow what you can do today'—that I went home and asked my boyfriend to leave."

"What did Garth say to that?"

"Nothing. He just told me I could go on to the second principle. That was three weeks ago."

"No shit?" Peter exclaimed. "How do you figure that guy?"

"You don't," she advised us. "I've met some of the students up on the seventh and eighth principles and they say that they still don't understand him. Some of them—I mean,

I don't think I'm any great shakes—but some of them seem even more screwed up than me. And they're nearly finished the training!"

Something inside me tightened and I felt like I'd been knocked on the head with a baseball bat. Lisa had all but verified that the whole training was a big scam. After eight months at two thousand dollars each, I would walk out of Xavier's house as big a basket case as when I had walked in. It was just like this world to pull a stunt like that; it was always finding some novel way to dump on me, and this time I had really been set up for it. It was like my father had always said: "Nothing ever changes."

"Well," Peter laughed heartily and slammed his hand down, shaking the glasses, "I've been conned a lot of times in my life—by some real pros—but I tell you, I've never enjoyed it so much! You gotta love the guy!"

"I do," Lisa admitted. "I think he's wonderful. And he hasn't conned me—he's giving me the whole course for free."

"What?" Cairn and I exclaimed in unison.

"I'm as surprised about it as you are. At first I thought he was putting the hit on me or something, and after a while I started hoping he would, but he just wants to...I don't know...give me this as a gift." By now my head was really swirling and not only did I not know what to think, at that moment I didn't know *how* to think.

"He sent you here, right?" Peter accused her.

"What? Why would he do that?"

"Sure, it's part of the con! He gets you to come in here and convince us that Garth Xavier is some kind of strange mystical being. First you bring up all our doubts and suspicions about this guy and then you blow them away—sure, I've seen that kind of thing lots."

"I don't know what you're talking about—why would he go to all that trouble?"

"Money."

"You think he's after your puny twenty thousand dollars."

"Sixteen," I corrected her.

"Whatever—he's charging other people twenty. Anyway, he's not in it for the money, believe me. Between him and his wife, they've got more money than a thousand students could give them."

"Well, maybe he's trying to get us into some kind of cult or something."

"I didn't know he was married," I mumbled, still trying to get my brain to start functioning again.

"A cult?" Jessica spoke up. "What decade are you living in?"

"It still happens," Peter insisted.

"Look," Lisa advised us, "maybe this kind of thing isn't for you—maybe it's too strange or something. But that's no reason to attack Garth. This is all about learning to live from your hearts; you'll never understand any of it if you keep coming from your heads. He could be any number of things according to your way of figuring it. But you'll never see what he has to offer you that way. This is a path of the heart. Maybe all those people I met on the seventh and eighth levels haven't understood that yet."

"Then what are they doing up there?" Peter wondered.

"Have you seen his wife?" I asked.

"I don't know—maybe because levels don't mean anything on this path—maybe because there's nothing to get or achieve. Who knows?"

"What d'you think, Jess?" Peter turned to the other woman.

"Don't ask me. I only met the man once, but nothing happened. Maybe he's not my type. But I'll tell you one thing: something must be okay about it—Lisa finally got rid of that jerk she was letting walk all over her."

"I still don't get it." Peter shook his head. "What's this guy about anyway? He looks like the father in some fifties TV show, uses some pretty weird strategies to get people into his school, charges them all differently, and teaches…what? What exactly are we learning?"

"If you don't know," Jessica inquired, "why are you going?" There was no reply from any of us, and the next few minutes were spent in relative silence. Why am I going, I asked myself repeatedly. What had been so attractive about the man that I had kept driving, week after week, to a dilapidated shack in the middle of nowhere, when I had not even the vaguest idea of what he had to offer? It simply did not make sense.

But then, what in my life ever had? All the regular

schooling, the menial summer and part-time jobs, the university nightmare, my counselling work, my marriage...my debt load...what was the purpose of it all? Was I really born for this; born onto a planet that was a virtual garden, just to plug into a dreary, ordinary routine?

I hope I'm wrong about this ...

"I'm going because it's true for me," I found myself saying. "I don't have any other explanation. And that's really new because I usually have an explanation for everything—some really rational justification."

"Me too," Peter agreed, although I didn't quite believe him.

"Me three!" Lisa joined in, and we all raised our glasses to toast our enigmatic teacher.

"To Garth Xavier, whoever the hell you are," Peter proclaimed.

THE WARRIOR'S THIRST

"Who am I?" the man smiled mysteriously. "Let's just say I'm an old friend, come to return a favour." It was good to see Garth, after the three weeks it had taken to complete my 'relationship assignment'. Peter had been seeing him regularly, having started a thing with Jessica that very night. I had not fared so well, since Lisa and I did not really hit it off, and I spent the next week in an envious fever over my friend, for whom everything always seemed to come so easily. I went into a bitter withdrawal, taking great pains to avoid him, until after a few days he confronted me in my office.

"Now what did I do?" he demanded.

"Nothing," I responded, not meeting his eyes. "I just haven't been feeling very good these last few days."

"Don't give me that crap, P.K. I know your face better than you do—I've had to look at it for years. You're pissed off at me because I'm going out with Jess, right? And because I get to go back and see Garth, right?"

"I'm not mad!" I disagreed irritably.

"Of course you're not. This is probably the way you

always look at work. I bet it really inspires confidence in your victims—I mean clients. Sure, they come in here, take one look at that face and realize they don't have it so bad after all."

"You're a funny man, Cairn," I said tiredly. "Maybe too funny. I'm not mad because of Jess or Garth; I'm just mad at how easy everything goes for you. Just like when we were in school—I'd do all the studying, and you'd just copy off of me."

"You never studied," my friend reminded me.

"I earned my marks by worrying a lot. One way or another I sweated for what I got, but you breezed through all of high school. And to top it off, you got better grades than me! It's always been that way, and I'm getting really tired of it."

"You know what your problem is, P.K.? You think you're better than me. You think that you deserve all kinds of good things more than I do because you're more spiritual, more intelligent, more together…you even think that Garth should like you more than me."

"No I don't," I objected lamely; Peter knew me too well.

"Sure you do. And you're going to do the same thing you do with every teacher or hero you get involved with; you're going to start talking like him and believing everything he says—Christ, if I know you, you'll even start walking like him!" Peter laughed, but I remained sullen. "Remember the time you were reading those Western novels—what were they called, the ones about that guy Buchanan? I saw you in the subway station one day and you were striding along like a real cowboy. You even had your hand hovering over your hip like you had a six-gun strapped to your side. It was the funniest bloody thing I ever saw!" Peter's heavy laughing rocked him back and forth and he slammed his hand down on my desk. Soon he was holding his sides, face beet red and eyes teary. It was too much for me as my sullen face broke into an embarrassed grin, and I chuckled softly.

"Hey, that was a long time ago, Cairn; I was seventeen."

"Oh, so you think you've changed now, right?" His laughter abated but the amused look on his face remained. "I've already seen you starting to emulate Garth, taking on his words and turning them into your new philosophy."

"It's not that. It's just that what he says really makes sense to me; it fits with the way I look at things. You have to admit it makes a lot of sense."

"What I've tried out for myself makes sense, but I don't take his word as gospel unless I see it and feel it for myself. You just soak up all the words and then act like you've got it all together, but you never practise any of it for yourself. I don't even think you really believe any of this stuff about the Warrior's Path—it's just something you can play with in your mind. And then you blame me because I get out there and try it."

"When did you get so smart?" I asked with friendly sarcasm.

"I hung around with a genius all my life," Peter replied.

As usual, we smoothed the matter out, but there was still a bad taste in my mouth. Putting it aside, I continued my assignment of 'opening up to receiving a partnership', as well as practicing the Warrior's Resolve in other areas. I watched my tendencies to procrastinate and short-circuited many of them by making a list of my daily priorities, and being sure to work from the top down. I also did my best to remain aware of where I was 'seconding myself' to the world, and found myself becoming angry and full of self-recrimination at how I'd let myself be a doormat. It had been in little things, like accepting a lukewarm meal in a restaurant—and then leaving my usual big tip. Losing my lunch hour to clients who went on talking past their time, or letting a salesperson talk me into buying something that I really didn't want. I wondered why I found it so hard to change these patterns, and vowed they would end. One of these days.

One outcome of my work with Garth, especially concerning my feelings about money, was that my clientele increased that very week. However, by the second week, the numbers had dropped again. I considered the possible causes and discovered that all the reasons I could think of fell under the 'shit happens' category. Then I tried Garth's technique and asked why I wouldn't *want* more clients (if I were to know). The immediate reply was, because I still viewed my work as a power drain; the more clients, the greater the drain. Since I didn't see my hard-work ethic disappearing in the near future, I came up with the inspiration to simply raise my rates. Karen, my secretary, questioned the wisdom of such a move until I mentioned her raise. It worked wonders for her attitude.

But still no mate. What made the endeavour even more

frustrating than it had been was the fact that Xavier had put the success of the assignment in my lap. Up until then, I had always looked at the mating scene as one that depended purely on chance. I just happened to be at the right place at the right time, said things that showed the woman my very best side and, since there was nothing better coming along for her, we hit it off. Sometimes, I would get that 'this is it' feeling. She was the one I had been looking for; I'm in love! et cetera, et cetera…. But over time those feelings changed for her, or me, or both of us, and we would go through an involved process of ending it. Who wanted to leave whom didn't matter. I always found myself alone, with the sneaking suspicion that it had been because of me, some deficiency life had given me. Or maybe it was the world that I didn't fit into. Or maybe it was that women wanted more than I was capable of giving—more than anyone could give. Whatever the reason, it was beyond me. By the time I got married, at the age of twenty-nine, I felt so inadequate as a partner that I had spent the entire relationship waiting for it to end. I just didn't believe it could work—and it wasn't my fault!

Then along comes Mr. Xavier, who says that the reality of this world is created by our beliefs. No wonder my sincere efforts to have a loving relationship met with failure. I believed that I had been cursed with some big unknowable thing which was totally unlovable. Even if I did beat the odds and find a woman who could tolerate my cynicism and low self-esteem, I would still be waiting for the other shoe to drop—the shoe with a nuclear warhead on its toe.

So it wasn't up to fate or some higher force to make it happen for me. According to Garth, having a successful relationship depended solely on my willingness to let one in. But how? That was the question nagging me for days while I wandered through libraries, museums, nightclubs and department stores. How do I become willing to have a partnership which I believe I'll destroy? Every time the statement, *I am willing to receive a mate,* entered my mind, I was overwhelmed with emotions that were anything but positive and willing. After nine days I dejectedly admitted defeat. Peter was right; I took in what Garth said, hoping that simply by assimilating the words, my life would be transformed, but I never really believed it. The heart of Garth's teachings were totally contrary to what I knew to be the truth about my life. Realizing that this meant I could not return to my training and that the only direction left seemed to be a continuation of my path of despair and emptiness, I considered ending my life. I was too fragile for this existence, too broken down by its relentless taunting of my mediocrity in a world where nice guys finished last and only cream and bastards floated to the top. Did I feel bitter and sorry for myself? Well, perhaps a little.

Instead of ending my life, I decided to make supper; I headed for the supermarket, feeling lost and frustrated. Maybe willingness only worked for people who had a stronger belief in themselves—people like Garth and Peter who had confidence and courage. I needed something more than willingness…a brain transplant, maybe. It was then that I happened to remember the second half of the Warrior's Discipline: the determination to let it happen. Great—more puzzles! Where exactly does one find that kind of determination. In my years of training, I had tried all kinds of techniques and gimmicks to improve my life or reach important goals— things like hypnosis, visualizations, affirmations and re-imaging, all the way to the other side of the spectrum, with tough emotional and mental confrontations in locked rooms with people and trainers who had all the compassion of army drill sergeants. None of these had any lasting effects that I could discern. They had helped with smaller concerns, but they never seemed to reach into the very centre of my belief. Either those beliefs were too powerful and would never be removed, or I had just never been really determined. But how determined does one have to be to let one's true self come forward? The answer that came was *determined enough*.

I am willing to receive, I am willing to receive, I am willing to receive….I kept repeating the mantra as I put food into my shopping cart, but this time not as an affirmation that blocked out any negative responses. Instead, I let the negative emotions continue to assault me, urging me to give up this silly charade. I felt them all, physically sickened by the despair and hopelessness of my beliefs. Amazed by how convincing those beliefs were, I was tempted to stop the process and run out to a movie or a drink, but instead I plunged into the very centre. Sometimes it was an anger, sometimes a deep, wailing sadness, and at first I would stop and close my eyes as each

new feeling surfaced in my consciousness. Each of these
emotions had a colour and a sound, and each was attached
to phrases that reflected a severely limiting belief that I had
been unknowingly carrying with me for years.

I am willing to receive, I am willing to receive...then
another mantra popped into my head, and as I plunged
deeper into the abyss of emotion, I repeated it: *I am not a
victim of the world I see*. What the hell, as my father used to
say, it's better than a kick in the teeth with a frozen boot!

After a few times, I no longer had to close my eyes when
another feeling emerged, but found that I could move into its
centre and dissolve it while picking out the items on my
shopping list. Suddenly I reached a mental wall that actually
seemed to hit me solidly in the chest. It was accompanied by
an impenetrable blackness and a sense of harsh disappointment, but the words that came from it had the matter-of-fact
tone of a colleague or close friend calmly informing me that
this was silly escapism. The fact of the matter, Patrick, is that
your life is ordinary because that's all you deserve. You're
lucky to get as much as you do out of it because, let's face it,
you're just not worth it. Beneath the disappointment was an
overwhelming sense of dis-confirmation. It reminded me of
one of the phrases a high school teacher had used on me
whenever I was acting up; he used to tell me, "You're not
worth the energy for me to go over there and smack you."

No wonder the techniques and gimmicks had never
worked. If I had possessed the self-worth that would have
made them effective, I probably wouldn't have needed the
gimmicks! Determination doesn't come from forcing it to be
there, nor does it arise from rigid mental discipline. It comes
from the realization that we're worth the constant effort. But
how could I believe I was worth a relationship, when I held
an overriding certainty that I wasn't? How could I be worth
being loved when there was so much mental and emotional
evidence to the contrary?

RESULTS = INTENTIONS

I heard Garth's voice, reminding me that if I didn't think
I had what I wanted, to set forth the intention to have it. All
of a sudden, I saw the importance of the assignment: Garth

didn't care if I had a relationship or not. He was using it to show me the importance of making myself the priority in my life: that I had the ability and the right to have anything I wanted, and that it was only me who was keeping it all out. Chasing after things only belied my belief that I didn't deserve to receive them unconditionally. If I truly became the priority, all the rest would naturally follow. Turn your back to the light, and you start chasing your shadow. Walk toward the light, and your shadow comes after you. In the blink of an eye, it seemed ludicrous to me that I should have spent so much time chasing after a relationship. Of course I could have a companion in my life; what was the big deal? It was a truly weird feeling, like some big weight had been removed and all of a sudden there was lots of space to play. What I had just understood made my entire pursuit of the woman of my dreams so unimportant. I had come into this life for some purpose that I would never find in the external world, and I was worthy of that purpose. Everything else would take care of itself. In the middle of the supermarket, while I waited to place my order for smoked salmon, I gave up to the invisible force of the universe my life-long obsession for the perfect woman.

I met Mira in the express line of the supermarket. It wasn't what I'd exactly call love at first sight, but there was some sort of tingling inside me when our eyes met, a kind of recognition followed almost immediately by the certainty that we would be together. Mira was new in town, so this offered me the perfect opportunity to do what I did best: eat. I was familiar with every restaurant in the city, and I could lead her anywhere to suit her palate, and follow it up with the specialty dessert of her choice. Mira was game, and for the first time in my life, everything else took care of itself.

The following days were a pleasant mixture of laughter and deep emotional exploration. In Mira I found a companion capable of delving into the strongest of feelings without fear or hesitation. The fear and hesitation were my department. While she stormed into the dusty rooms of my wounded past relationships, I followed behind, nervously requesting that she not look over there, and leave that file alone.

"Tell me about you and Darlene," she requested after we had finished our veal parmigiano at my favourite Italian restaurant.

"Not much to tell," I stated matter-of-factly, although I almost winced at the sharp pain in my chest.

"Do you still love her?"

"Did I ever love her—that's the question."

"No, that's the Pat Kennedy way of avoiding a question."

"Love is such a strange word. It can mean anything from strong preference to insane jealousy. Whatever I felt for my ex-wife, whether it was love or not, got lost in the routine of coping."

"I hope someone evicts you pretty soon from that penthouse apartment of yours," Mira stated, playfully throwing a parsley stalk at my head. "There are no feelings up there!"

"But I don't like what I feel down here." I thumped my chest. "Yeah, I still love her, but what's that got to do with anything? If I let myself feel it, it would tear me up; then I'd be no good for anyone or anything."

"What are you going to do—stay up in your head until the feeling wanders off? What good are you doing anyone up there?"

"At least I can remain objective until time takes the pain down a notch or two. How could I help my clients if I was wrapped up in suffering while they're trying to clear their lives up—they need a cool head in their crises."

"They need someone to be there with them, P.K., not yelling down to them from that tower you're hiding in."

"Who's hiding? I'm not hiding. I just don't see—"

"You don't want to see, you mean. Anyone can teach people to run from their pain—this culture's been doing it for years. But Patrick, you could give people so much more. You could help them get their feelings back."

"I don't know if I would exactly call that help, Mira. I don't know if you've noticed, but a lot of those feelings hurt like a son of a bitch. You just say 'Darlene', and I feel like you've stabbed me."

"Why didn't you tell me that?" she demanded angrily.

"Hey, don't get upset. I just—"

"I am upset! You told me last night that you really cared for me, and that you wanted to be with me. Well, be with me!"

"I am," I reasoned, awkwardly aware of the attention we were receiving from the other patrons. "It's just that…well, shit Mira, no one's ever wanted that from me before. No

girlfriend, anyway," I added, thinking of Garth. "Every relationship I've ever been in has had me trying to figure out what
the heck my partner wanted and giving it to them before they
got sick of waiting. Air-traffic controllers have had less stress
in their lives than I've had in my relationships. I've run around
like a crazy man trying to give them what I thought they
wanted, and they all ended up being disappointed in me. It's
never been enough." Tears appeared in my eyes, and I felt
ashamed of myself.

"You feel like a failure, don't you?" she said quietly.

"What was your first clue?"

"Don't," she pleaded sincerely. "Don't shut me out with
that fake humour. Machismo doesn't become you. It doesn't
become anyone."

"I'm sorry," I responded, brushing the tears away quickly.
"I didn't mean to lay this on you."

"Don't be sorry. I can feel you with me now."

"Why would you want to see this crap? Imagine if every
time we got together I started wailing and crying about what
a loser I am. Who needs it?"

"You really think that that's you, don't you?"

"No, but—"

"Yes, you do. You think that the best part of you is in your
head, and that everything else below is either too ugly, or a
waste of time. To tell you the truth, the feelings you just
showed are a lot more attractive to me than anything that
could fall out of that penthouse of yours. And I hate to be the
one to break this to you, but I'm pretty sure that most women
feel the same way I do."

"You like to see all men as failures," I jibed, but Mira didn't
go for the bait.

"I like to see men being men: facing their emotions and
their rawness with sensitivity and courage."

"I dunno, Mira. I really don't know if I can do this.
Sometimes I don't feel anything. I might as well be an android
for all the emotions I feel in touch with. This may be one more
excuse, but I grew up in a pretty rough place. My old man used
to take turns drinking up his pay cheque and tormenting us.
We were never allowed to show any strong feelings—my
mother told us that it would upset him. And the neighbourhood was even worse. I can't ever remember a time that I

didn't leave the house wondering if I was going to get beat up. Showing any kind of feelings was just asking for trouble; the gangs would kill you for being a fag if they saw you being emotional. Being smart was what saved my ass! And then girls! They all wanted someone strong and cocky, and ready to fight for them at the drop of a hat."

"To top it all off, somewhere deep inside me I believe that I'm the cause of it all. I feel like there's something very dark and bad in me that brings nothing but shit and despair into people's lives, and I don't know if I can change."

"I don't want you to change, P.K. I want you to be you— all of you. I don't just want to see your best, or what you think is your best; showing just that one side can get boring really fast. I want to feel things with you. To go into our dark sides together and see if it's really as terrible as we think it is."

"I don't know, Mira." I shook my head and looked down at the table as the tears welled up again. "I feel like I'm going to let you down like I have everyone else. And I don't think I could stand facing that kind of disappointment again."

"Well then, we can feel the disappointment together and see if it kills us. God, do you want to live in fear forever? I don't." She punched me on the shoulder playfully. "What do you say—do you want to get really naked?" I lifted up my head to meet her playful gaze, her simplicity and innocence causing a fresh flow of tears to leak out. Was I really getting another chance to live my life in a better way? Would she, would anyone stay with me through all the hurt and ugliness that I carried within? Would I stay with Mira through hers? Could I stand to look at myself so openly? Could I truly, successfully get naked with someone and live to talk about it?

"Why not," I shrugged, wondering why it always took me so long to realize that I had nothing to lose. "Let's start at your place."

"Start what?"

"Getting naked," I responded as I watched her pay the bill.

"You're just after me for sex," she accused me, smiling.

"Oh no," I objected. "I want your money, too!"

✦

Things went so well after that night that it was another week before I even thought of Garth Xavier. At that, if I hadn't given him the money already, I wondered if I ever would have returned.

"Oh, you would have been back," Xavier assured me. "You're destined to be a warrior." We were no longer in the small study, now that there were a half-dozen other people in the class. We sat in chairs to form a semi-circle with Garth facing us. Other than the easel and a small table with water on it, the room was bare, but warm.

"You have what is called the Warrior's Thirst. Because you were doomed to forget who you really are as soon as you came into this world, there was placed inside you a thirst for the Truth. As hard as we all try to quench that thirst by various offerings from the world, nothing ever quite does it. You would never be satisfied, Patrick, by anything the world has to offer you: no wealth, no achievements, and no great romantic involvement. Truth won't stop you from trying to find satisfaction in the illusion. It knows that you just won't be satisfied with less than your true destiny."

"How come I never felt it?" I asked

"Everyone feels the thirst; its subtlety is often ignored, that's all. One of the biggest blocks in your life has been your expectations. You've always looked for some big, exciting phenomenon to come into your life…some kind of magic. It's a common failing of those who claim to be on a spiritual path. They try to measure their progress by phenomena—like walking on water, changing the weather…invoking some god, or levitating—fantastic things."

"What's wrong with that?" a woman asked. "I've read about monks in India who practise those things all the time—and their whole lives are spent in spiritual matters."

"There's nothing wrong with magic. But it's no big deal either."

"Can you do magic?" two other students spoke simultaneously.

"I have my moments," the teacher responded mysteriously. "Look, those kinds of things are really no big deal. They're all fine to play with, under the right guidance, but they're still just phenomena. As such, they're of this world and therefore, not the Truth."

"Well," the only other male student besides Peter and me spoke up in a complaining tone, "what the heck are we here to learn? I thought spiritual warriors played with time and space and the elements and ethers…controlling the weather and stuff like that. What are we supposed to be learning from you?"

"Why would you want to control the weather, Henry?"

"I don't know. Just, you know…so I could see how powerful I am. You told me when I first met you that I wasn't letting my true power come out, so I thought you were going to show me stuff like that."

"Okay," the teacher rose from his seat and walked over to the door, opened it and turned to face us. "Let's go out back." The atmosphere in the room had shifted subtly, as many of us exchanged looks that said, finally we're getting to the real stuff! I was a little nervous as we followed him out to his patio. Beyond its shelter, the huge lawn was being lightly sprinkled by a cold late-autumn rain. "Now Henry, would you like me to teach you how to stop this rain?" the teacher addressed the young fair-haired man, who seemed to be in his late teens or early twenties.

"Sure," Henry stated enthusiastically.

"Good. Now are you ready to take on the karma of your act?"

"What d'you mean?"

"You can't just change one thing without affecting everything else. You have to be willing to accept responsibility for your choices."

"Well…" the young man stammered, "like…what could happen?"

"Who knows?"

"I thought maybe we could just…you know…just change it right here in the yard. Just for a minute or two."

"Yeah," I joined in good-naturedly, "How about hanging a cute little rainbow or two right up there in front of us?" A few of the students laughed politely.

"Sure," Garth nodded agreeably. "You just be willing to take on the karma and I'll show you how. Look, everything is connected to everything else in this universe. Every decision you make affects the whole. You can do anything, absolutely anything you want to, as long as you're willing to accept the consequences of every single choice. Now, you're making choices constantly in your life. Most of them are the same subconscious choices you've been making every day for years—and look at the results. How would you rate them?"

"Terrible!" this pronouncement came from Marietta and Lyette, the same two who had spoken in unison before. They looked at each other in surprise and then laughed with embarrassment.

"So before you decide to take on the big hardware, how about mastering the software first?" We all agreed that this was a good idea and returned to our room, but before I went back inside the house, I turned to look again at the yard. My mouth dropped at what I saw: a tiny opening appeared impossibly in the thick dark clouds and two faint rainbows made their presence visible. I looked away to whisper a call to my friend, but when I looked again, the clouds had closed so completely that I immediately doubted what I had witnessed. Garth materialized behind me and said quietly, "So many beautiful experiences get lost in the attempt to prove their validity. Don't worry—I'll show you how to do it too—some day."

I gulped, but found the strength to voice my fear. "What kind of karma do I get for that?"

"That one's on me," he offered, putting his arm around my shoulder.

"Thanks," I said humbly.

"That's what friends are for." It seemed then that time stood still, and all I was aware of were his infinitely deep eyes, as we stopped in the long hallway and he stood facing me.

"Are you really my friend?"

"I'm your true friend, Patrick. I promise you right here and now. And there is no place you can go that I won't come to get you when you call."

"I'd really like to believe that, Garth," I declared, as tears welled up behind my eyes. "I need to believe it. But I'm scared."

"Don't worry," he said soothingly, "you have friends in high places, and they want you back. I'm committed to that." I felt like I was in a dream as I followed him back into the room. There was a comforting sensation in my chest that reminded me of the night when I had felt so completely loved

from within. I wanted to ask him about that experience—
whether or not it really had been his voice I heard, but not in
front of the class. For now it was enough to feel the love
coming from him, and to watch him turn and give the same
to the others. I wondered how it was possible for anyone to
love so much.

We spent the rest of the morning and early afternoon
learning how to reach that love, sometimes through his direct
teaching, and at other times through personal process. Using
a variety of techniques, Garth penetrated our subconscious
minds, as we discovered places within where pain had been
stored for a long, long time. It was then left up to us: choose
forgiveness or hold onto the pain. The fascinating part of the
method was that he did not have to interact directly with me
for the process to be effective. Either by involving myself in
the other person's story, or by following my own while Garth
asked someone else questions that easily applied to me, I
experienced great depths of emotion, both painful and
curative. It was amazing how many harmful choices were
haunting me to the present day, and how difficult it seemed
to choose again with any conviction, so convinced was I that
what had been done was unchangeable.

I watched how the others responded to Garth, wondering
how they perceived this enigmatic man. It was obvious by
their attentiveness that they respected him, but in some of the
students' eyes, I thought,I saw more. Some of them seemed
in awe of his every word and action, while others actually
appeared fearful whenever he addressed them.

I decided to bring the subject up at the next break when
the teacher wasn't around. All eight of us sat at a round
wooden table under the shelter of Garth's backyard gazebo,
drinking coffee and munching on the teacher's home-made
cookies, which were surprisingly tasty. A light drizzle continued to fall as I put forth the question, who is Garth Xavier
really?

"I think he's wonderful," Vivian stated. "I think he's a real
saint."

"Yeah, he's pretty wild alright." Peter nodded his head,
then shook it. "But I'm not so sure about the saint stuff; he's
just a normal guy who has his trip together is all I see."

"Normal?" I blurted incredulously. "That man is far from

normal!"

"So what are you saying—that he's some kind of special soul?"

"Isn't that obvious?"

"Only to those with putty for brains."

"I think he's a very good, wise, and kind man who wants to help the world out of its pain," Beverly pitched in.

"I heard that he used to be some kind of guru in California," Vivian added.

"I think he's Jesus," Henry stated flatly, and this stopped us short. "He said he would come again, didn't he? And Garth fits everything I ever read about Christ." Like a child expecting some grownup to break in and punish us, I found my body bracing itself, waiting for the bolt of lightning that would shatter the gazebo, leaving the charred remains of eight bodies twisted into the word BLASPHEMERS.

"Uh, Hank..." Peter broke the silence. "Maybe you'd better go have a lie-down. Did you bring your blanky with you?"

"He could be!" Marietta interjected. "Look at the man— he's so pure, so full of love and forgiveness. He's obviously experiencing God."

"Hey, let's not get carried away here," Lyette, Marietta's companion, advised us. "I think Garth is a really wonderful man too, but if you guys put him on a pedestal, you won't be able to reach him."

"Yeah," Peter agreed. "That's probably what they did with J.C. too! For all we know he could have been a regular guy, y'know? Hanging out with gangsters and chasing broads—"

"Peter!" Vivian was shocked.

"Sorry. I mean women."

"That's not what I meant. You can't talk about Jesus like that. It's...disrespectful."

"Hey, Jesus doesn't mind."

"Look, we were talking about Garth, remember?" I spoke up nervously. We were in dangerous territory as far as I was concerned. As little involvement as I had with religion, equating Garth with Jesus seemed like a bad idea. What were they seeing that I wasn't? "I just wanted to know what you thought about him, who you think he is."

"What difference does it make?" Lyette asked.

"Don't worry about Kennedy," Cairn chuckled. "He just wants to know if he's going to be imitating the right guy." The woman smiled and continued.

"He's a loving man who's offering you the chance to win your heart back, giving you the opportunity to forgive people you never thought you could, and enjoy life more fully. What does it matter who he is?"

"Jim Jones offered the same thing," Marlene put in. "You have to be careful about giving your power away to someone just because they talk like a holy person."

"So what are you saying—that Garth might be evil? All he talks about is truth, love, forgiveness...how could that be bad?"

"Even the Devil quotes the Bible," Marlene shot back defensively.

Peter groaned. "Christ! Are you getting enough oxygen there, lady?" He was being more obnoxious than usual, a sure sign that he was nervous about something. Maybe he liked Garth more than he wanted to admit.

"I don't find you very funny, Peter! Patrick asked for our opinions and I gave mine. Just because I didn't say 'Baaaa' like the rest of the sheep..."

"Anytime you people are ready," Garth called from the patio. We all turned to look at him, our minds churning with doubt and unformed questions. I trailed behind the group as we walked back to the classroom. It seemed that every time I began to feel closer to Garth a new wave of uncertainty would hit me, and I would be torn between the desire—no, the need—to be accepted and loved by him, and the fear that my trust would be betrayed, and I would never recover from the hurt. It occurred to me, with a sharp pain, that this was how I experienced all intimate relationships. The whole time I had been with Darlene, I had wanted her to come closer while waiting for her to reject me. How could she have stood it for so long, being constantly treated like a threat or potential enemy? *I'm so sorry*, I muttered to her while I walked down the hall, *I never meant to hurt you like that—please forgive me.* I vowed that I wouldn't let this addiction to mistrust come between me and Mira. She deserved more than to have her offer of love met with haunting paranoia. I would claw my way through it if I had to. I would take the risk and trust her;

she deserved at least that much. Taking a seat, I felt much lighter inside, and my questions regarding Mr. Xavier faded away. For my own sake I would trust him, and I would know him by his gifts.

✧

"You're missing the point, Patrick. You've been holding on to this pain because you think you were pushed away, and this holding on is a form of revenge."

"I can't change that," I argued, "I was pushed away. It happened. Just by imagining the picture changing doesn't change the facts."

"Are you sure it happened the way you think it did?"

"As best as I can tell—that's what it feels like anyway. I'm just putting what I remember about my parents and my family into a scene you've told me to make up. So now I see me as a little baby, alone in my crib. I'm crying and my mother walks in and tries to feed me. When that doesn't work, she changes my diapers, walks around holding me and singing, and then after awhile she gets fed up and leaves. And then I get scared and scream even louder, so she comes back and slams the door on me. That's what she was like sometimes—I can't change that. And it hurt me. I can't change that either."

"Okay, now let's play a little game," the teacher suggested. "Let's just say that you wanted it to happen that way. What was its affect on you?"

"I dunno …I guess I was terrified."

"Were you?"

"I guess so—I was only a little kid."

"Check it out," he urged me, "keep looking at that baby and tell me about the feeling he's experiencing." I did as I was directed as best I could. It was easier now that I was no longer feeling self-conscious about the others. All of them, even Peter, had bared their souls to some extent, one always going a little deeper than the previous.

"Oh! He's not scared—he's pissed off!"

"And the reason for his anger is…?"

"It's a lot more than mere anger, Garth. This baby wants

to kill!"

"And the reason for that is...?"

"Because my mother walked out on me."

"I sense that he was enraged before she left," Xavier corrected me.

"That's true," I admitted, my eyes still closed and viewing the inner play. I was impressed by the ferociousness of my rage.

"And the reason you were so pissed off in the first place was...?"

"I was mad at her for bringing me here," I blurted, suddenly feeling the ire toward my mother rush through my thirty-three-year-old body.

"So what you decided to do was...?"

"I wanted to make her pay. But that doesn't make sense! How could a little baby hate so much—they're too innocent."

"Maybe that's where you lost your innocence and took on your victimhood," Garth suggested.

"But I *was* the victim. It was me who got left." The rage burned through me and I felt a deep hatred for everyone in the room. It would soon spread even further, I was sure.

"And what was the result of her leaving?"

"I got madder. What a bitch—just walking out on me like that."

"And what did your mother feel?"

"Nothing," I stated flatly. "How could anyone with feelings ever leave a little baby to cry like that?"

"Nothing? Go a little deeper and check it out."

"Actually," I admitted, "she's feeling terrible. She's in her room crying."

"And what's making her cry? What kind of feeling?"

"Guilt—she believes she's a terrible mother. She feels bad about not being able to help me."

"So did she leave you or did you push her out of the room with your rage?"

"I pushed her," I admitted, tears once again rising. "I was getting back at her for bringing me into this shitty world. I never wanted to be here!"

"Spoken like a true victim," Peter acknowledged, imitating the teacher. There was some laughter.

"So," Garth continued, "Your revenge on your mom was

aimed at making her feel like a terrible mother. Good work."

"But it hurt me worse!" I insisted.

"Of course, revenge has a way of doing that."

"But even knowing that, there's still something inside me that doesn't want to let her off the hook. She should have known better!"

"So what was she feeling that didn't let her know better?"

"What? I don't understand."

"Just see her crying in her room—what's going on inside of her, underneath the guilt?" I concentrated for over a minute as the others sat quietly, either involved in their own inner worlds, or else looking into mine.

"She's feeling helpless," I replied at length.

"And have you ever felt helpless in your life?" Garth asked.

"Sure. I must have."

"Do you remember any time when you felt what your mother felt?" His question immediately brought to mind a particularly difficult time with my daughter Maya, one night when she absolutely refused to go to sleep. I was alone with her and at my wits' end. My utter helplessness put me on the brink of wanting to throw her out the window.

"Yeah, I can remember," I informed him.

"Can you feel that feeling now—the helplessness, I mean?"

"Yeah, a little bit."

"Can you understand how your mother felt?"

"Yeah," I whispered.

"Can you forgive her for feeling the way she did? And stop punishing her for it? She was just like you, Patrick—lost and helpless, with no one to turn to for help. Can you see the spot she was in, and forgive her?"

> *Mother, you always did your best,*
> *Mother, you never stopped for rest*
> *What love did you possess that you*
> *Could give to us the whole day through?*

Without opening my eyes I could discern that the melodic, solitary voice was not far from the room. It was female, and reminded me of when I was a child and my mother would sing as she performed her household chores.

> *Mother, I never understood*
> *Mother, I doubt I ever could*
> *You loved me 'til your dying day*
> *And ne'er expected me to say*
>   *Thank you*

It was too much for me. The beauty of the voice and the song made me realize that I was aching to love my mother, and the wall that had held back years of unspent tears began to crumble. I saw her in my mind: a fragile soul beset by a life she had been unprepared for. I looked inside her and perceived the disappointment that she could not do better for us, and the guilt of having failed us as a mother. And suddenly I realized that I had been carrying inside me the same judgments of myself: that I had failed her as a son, that I had not been there for her, not been good enough. Again I felt enraged at life for dealing me a poor hand. Xavier must have seen it in my face—or mind—because he urged me on.

"Don't stop there—just keep going," he insisted. I tried, but the anger was unbearable. My body tensed as I endured the raw hatred coursing through my veins. I could taste venom in my mouth, and I wanted to howl like a rabid animal. The rage swirled about me and through me, but I couldn't think of anyone to vent it against. In the back of my mind was a calm, rational voice that suggested, quite innocuously, that my veins were about to explode. *Keep going Patrick; this is no place to stop and have a picnic.* And then I was howling. The sounds ripped from my throat were like no animal's I had ever heard. Vaguely, I remember thrashing about on the floor while hands did their best to restrain me, and I was loudly reminded not to hurt myself. At the time, the warning seemed completely ludicrous—what physical injury could match the pain that was racking my insides? For no reason I can recall, I heard myself praying silently, an inner voice calling for help, and the intense rage changed immediately to that utter helplessness I had experienced earlier in my infant self. I opened my eyes and stared, gaping at the bodies hovering above me. I just barely recognized Peter, but did not really know who he was, while the rest, including Xavier, were complete strangers to me. I didn't feel afraid, but neither was I at a place of peace. I was simply aware of the utter helplessness of my condition—trapped inside a body that could barely move. I was strongly tempted to revert to my previous state of hateful rage, but a soothing voice from outside of me seemed to deter me. I did not understand the words, but I did comprehend the intent behind them. I continued to call for help, and that's when everything disappeared.

Or, I should say, that was when everything appeared. It was as though the bodies around me were like huge costumes that fell away to reveal who the people inside really were. Then the costumes were back on…then they were off again. It was as if I had a view of two distinct worlds, with a foot in each. In one world, everyone was pure luminescence and, as I looked at the lights, I could feel that they were all interconnected. Then I would shift my awareness to the other side and see the bodies. There was no indication that they were in any way connected to one another. The human forms seemed to emanate an energy of suffering, and when I directed my awareness toward them, I also suffered. As I redirected my attention to the other world, I felt peaceful.

"One of these days I'm going to understand what the hell is going on." The sound of Peter's voice brought me back to reality—or at least to what I had taken for reality all these many years. Helping hands pulled me up and I returned to my chair, feeling like a rag doll or boneless chicken.

"Welcome home," Xavier said, the mischievous glint in his eyes letting me know that he knew.

"Thank you," I said, then turned to the rest of the group. "Thanks guys." They responded heartily, all saying, in various ways, good work. I turned back to Xavier. "Now what just happened?"

"Well, from the looks of you, I'd say you faced your pain, and chose forgiveness over revenge. Why don't you tell us what happened?" I described it as best I could, and found that even as I described the other world, the actual feelings that I had experienced there became vague, so much that I questioned whether it had been real. When I finished, Garth went over to the easel and printed in huge letters that took up the whole page:

There is only one problem.

He stopped to make eye contact with each of us, then turned the sheet over the top and printed on the fresh page:

That problem is separation.

The next page:

From that problem all other

Next page:

problems come.

"What you discovered, Patrick, was a solution to every problem you have. To whatever depth you went, you saw that there would be no problems if you looked at the world as it truly is. It's your choice—to perceive separation—that is the cause of all your unhappiness. To maintain separation is very painful, so you have to bury the hurt, keeping it suppressed by your anger or denial. Anger and blame are great ways to reject your pain, but in rejecting your pain you reject yourself." He looked around the class.

"What allowed this experience to happen was that Patrick quit blaming his mother and faced the long-buried hurt inside him. His willingness to go through the pain took him right out of the subconscious into deeper, more powerful realms of the mind. These are the deepest waters I've ever gone with anyone on the first principle. Good work, Patrick."

"My friend!" Peter declared proudly, "The Jacques Cousteau of Warriors!"

"All pain," Garth continued, "began with the initial separation. Every time you choose not to run from your pain, but to address it without defense or anger, you will see that..." he went to the easel again:

Pain is not real!

"—pain isn't real. It's merely the idea that you are fragmented or separated from yourself."

"How's that?" Lyette inquired. "It feels pretty real to me. And Patrick seemed pretty convinced of it too, judging by the way he was rolling around there."

"Only love is real," Garth explained. "Don't get me wrong, I go through a lot of pain in my life. But my experience tells me that forgiveness is greater. Love, compassion, truth, inspiration...they can heal any hurt. By wanting love more than the hurt, you integrate the energy of the pain into the higher vibration of the love. You retrieve a part of yourself, and the hold on your belief in separation is lessened; you glimpse what masters through the ages have been trying to show us: I am not this body."

"But how do I stay there?" I asked.

"Want to," the teacher replied simply.

"I did want to, but something drew me back."

"Oh? And what might that have been?"

"Peter's voice."

"Hey, don't blame it on me, man; I've got enough guilt as it is."

"I'm not blaming you—I'm just saying that something in your voice called me back."

"It's what is called misguided loyalty," Garth informed us.

"What, because of my loyalty to Peter I gave up...my happiness?"

"No, because of your loyalty to this world. Your loyalty to hard work, to blood, sweat, and tears, your loyalty to a conspiracy of revenge against life." The teacher returned to his chair, "Your loyalty to the separation."

"That's all in my voice?" Peter asked, but I didn't wait for Garth's reply.

"That's crazy."

"True," the teacher agreed. "But when has that stopped you before?"

"I don't believe it—it's just impossible," I insisted.

"Well," Garth shrugged, "just look at the results; results equal intentions."

"How do you know? You say this is all our choosing, that I've got my problems and my suffering because I chose them—even because I wanted them. But for all I know, that could just be your belief...how do you know?"

"Tell me this first," he suggested. "Why are you being so petulant right now?"

"I dunno." My shoulders sagged. "I just feel like I got kicked out again."

"Again?"

"That just slipped out. But I really wanted to stay there,

and then you said it was my decision to leave. It just felt to me that it wasn't—that somebody or something decided for me. Either way I can't win…and I can't go back there—wherever 'there' is."

"Let's go with the first hypothesis: that you were kicked out. Now, who do you think kicked you out?"

"I dunno…God, I guess…whatever that means."

"What does God mean to you?"

"You know…God. The omniscient, omnipresent, omnipotent…whatever…energy or power, or whatever."

"So why would a being like that kick you out?"

"You tell me. Maybe he's crazy, or cruel or something. Maybe I did something wrong and he got pissed off at me."

"You mean this being punished you for doing something wrong? Tell me Patrick, is your God a loving God, a hateful God, or something else—a fickle God, maybe?"

"Well, if he really was God, he'd have to be a loving God," I replied.

"So would your God be all-loving, or loving just part of the time?"

"Naturally he'd have to be all-loving."

"Then why would an all-loving God kick you out of your home?"

"Well, like I said, maybe I did something wrong and he's punishing me."

"What could you have done that was so wrong it would affect perfect love in any way?"

"Maybe he's punishing me because it's for my own good—"

"Ah!" Garth interjected, "Now you're defending him."

"No, I'm not. I'm just saying maybe love does punish—I'm not saying it's right, I'm just saying maybe that's the way it is."

"Why would something perfect punish you with separation. It doesn't recognize separation. Constancy can't punish just sometimes—perfection doesn't change. And what wrong might you commit that perfect love couldn't immediately undo? What is perfect love not capable of?"

"Maybe God's not perfect!" I countered desperately.

"How could love not be perfect? It wouldn't be love if it wasn't perfect. God wouldn't be God if he, or she, or it wasn't all loving. Whatever mistake you made, wouldn't it have been forgiven immediately?"

"Then, how come I can't go home? If I'm forgiven, what's the problem?"

"Funny," Garth said, "I was just about to ask you that!"

"The problem is that I don't feel forgiven."

"Why not? If that pure and perfect love has forgiven you, is giving you the green light to come home, why don't you let yourself feel it?"

"Because I can't!" I exclaimed.

"You can't, or you don't want to? You were there awhile ago. Why didn't you just stay there?"

"I told you—they wouldn't let me."

"Oh, so now it's they," Garth said teasingly.

"I don't know why I said that," I admitted.

"Just for the fun of it," the teacher suggested, "let's replace the words 'I can't' with 'I don't want to'. Now I know, I know, you really do want to. But just for the fun of it—just to humour me—let's say you didn't want to stay there. Why would that be?"

"I can't even imagine an answer," I replied steadfastly.

"Aw c'mon, just play along with me, Pat; you love playing games! If I were to know the reason I didn't want to stay in the light, it would be because…?"

"Because I'm still mad at it?" I guessed.

"I'm still mad at it because…?"

"Because it kicked me out."

"I thought we already covered that." Xavier rubbed his chin. "Perfect love doesn't reject."

"Okay, okay," I said, beginning to enjoy myself. The guy was right—I did love playing games. "So I screwed up somehow and God forgave me immediately. Only I didn't think he did, so I…left?"

"Great! So you left because you didn't feel forgiven and, as most guilty people do, you blamed God for kicking you out."

"Wait a minute—I didn't get that last part," Peter interrupted.

"Guilt is like an acid that eats away at us. When we're not ready to forgive, the alternative is to try and throw it onto somebody else—by blaming them for what we think we really did to ourselves. Patrick felt so guilty about whatever it was

he did, that even though the pure love forgave him immediately—"

"I wasn't willing to forgive myself!" I finished for him. "I
felt so bad that I left, and just so I could feel better, I made it
all God's fault."

"How does that sound to you?" Xavier questioned me,
"Does it make sense?"

"No," I stated honestly, "but it does sound like something
I would do."

"But what could anyone do that would cause all this
trouble?" Peter wondered.

"Well, Peter, let's just say that the essential ingredient of
being home is that you're happy, okay?"

"How do we even know that?"

"By our basic motivating force. Everybody is motivated by
the desire to feel good—would you agree?"

"Well," my friend hedged, "I don't know about everybody, but I know that it's what motivates me."

"And what would cause you to feel unhappy?"

"A lot of things," Peter responded. "Not enough sex, no
money, no friends...."

"Yeah, yeah," Xavier interrupted gently. "But at the root
of all those things—what is the essential cause of being
unhappy: without which, all the sex, drugs, and money would
just be so many empty experiences?"

"Not being at home?" Henry guessed.

"That's too simple," Cairn said, condescendingly.

"That's right on, Henry," Xavier stated.

"Yeah, good catch there, Hank!" Peter commended him,
turning a full one-eighty. The teacher continued.

"So let's say that being home means being happy. Then
it would follow that being unhappy means not being home.
Not being home means...?"

"Separation?"

"And where would we find the root of that separation?"

"In our minds?" Henry said hesitantly.

"In our minds," Peter repeated as though he was the first
one to think of it.

"So what you did that was so wrong was...?"

"We thought about separation," I deduced.

"Right! You conceived of the possibility that you could

somehow be separate from home—or from God, depending on how you want to look at it. Then you believed your fantasy was real."

"When you say you, do you mean me?" I asked.

"No, I mean we."

"So you mean you," I teased him.

"No, I mean you," Garth returned pointedly. "The rest of us are a product of your choosing to believe in separation. How could you see separate bodies if you had no concept of separation?"

"Yeah, but everyone else here sees individual bodies or people," I argued.

"Only because you do," he countered, smiling. "Remember what I said at your first class: Warriors know they are responsible for everything that happens in their lives, because everything that is outside a Warrior is a reflection of an internal process, consisting of picture, feeling and thought. If you hold the thought of separation, the pictures and feelings inside will respond accordingly, and these are what you project outwardly. That is, if you think separation, you'll see separation."

"You mean," I said doubtfully, "this is all in my mind?" I waved my arms to encompass the room and then pointed to myself. "All of this room is inside here?"

"No, even your body is a reflection; in a sense, your mind isn't in your body—your body is in your mind. Don't you remember what you just told us happened to you, Patrick? When your mind thought of unity, you saw us all connected in the light; and when you thought of separation, you saw us all as separate bodies, suffused with problems and suffering. That is what you told us, isn't it?"

"Yeah," I answered, my voice full of doubt, "but right now, I feel like I just imagined the whole thing. I'm not sure it really happened at all."

"That's what happens. When you're here, home seems like a mere dream—an impossible dream at that. And when you're home...when you're in heaven, this place is the dream."

"So now that we know this, why can't we just go back?" Peter wondered.

"You can," Garth assured him. "The question is, why don't you want to?"

"Because I don't really believe it?"

"Even the beliefs we hold are of our own choosing. Patrick, why did you choose not to stay in the light?"

"I swear I don't know, Garth."

"You seem to have gone there fairly easily; why don't you just go there again?"

"I don't know how I did it—it was like it just happened."

"I believe you, but you must have somehow let it happen—what was it you did?"

"Nothing, I just asked for help and then something took over," I explained.

"You mean—" Garth stopped dramatically, and looked at me with overstated awe, his sparkling eyes wide open, "—you mean, you let go of your control?" He wrote on the easel:

GUILT	JUDGEMENT
BLAME	REVENGE
ANGER	SACRIFICE
RAGE	INDULGENCE
FEAR	HABITS/PATTERNS

"These are some of the major ways we try to control our lives—the ways in which we keep ourselves from being free and happy. As a matter of fact, when we're not happy and loving, we're trying to control our lives. As soon as you ask for help—sincerely, and not out of habit—you set forth an intention to let go of trying to control your life; no sincere call for help will go unanswered."

"How do you know if you're being sincere or not?" Beverly asked. I was so absorbed in the process I had forgotten about the others in the room.

"By the results! You're sincere if you're willing to ask for help, and then…let the Grace help you. It was Patrick's wanting the Truth so much that he gave up trying to control that allowed the help to come. But even his wanting the Truth at that moment came by Grace."

"But that makes it all pretty iffy!" the woman declared. "What you're saying is that none of this is in our hands at all! I feel like we're right back where we started. Like we're victims of some Divine Whimsy. You're saying that I'm not free because I don't want to be, but I can only want to be if the Grace lets me want it. We really are helpless."

"Right. But you think you're not helpless, and you prove that thought by trying to control your lives. The key is in realizing your helplessness."

"But how can I realize that?"

"By wanting to. The problem is not with the inconsistency of the Grace—all perfection is constant. The problem is with what keeps us from constantly wanting the Grace to lead us back home. We are the fickle ones. We are the ones with the free will; we can either want to go home or want to remain separate. Patrick has free will. Even when he was back home in the light, he could still choose to leave, simply by imagining separation, and attaching himself to that thought—using the illusory familiarity of Peter's voice as an anchor."

"But why would he want to do that?" Bev persisted.

"Funny," Garth feigned confusion, scratching his head, "I thought I asked that about twenty minutes ago. We're still waiting for your answer, Patrick. You were willing to glimpse the real world, you just weren't willing to stay there—and you're not willing to go back there now, because...? If you were to know...?"

"I don't know; I just...I guess I just don't feel like I deserve anything that beautiful." I shuffled uncomfortably at my admission, realizing I could no longer fully justify my anger at God, life, and the rest of the known universe. "I really don't feel like I'm worth it."

"Now that's a Warrior's answer—responsible and honest. To the best of his knowledge, that is. As long as you remain aware of that unworthiness, and keep choosing to be free of it, the Grace of the Universe will take care of the rest. Time can heal all wounds." Then he added playfully, "Or wound all heals!"

"But how much time is it going to take?" Cairn demanded. "We could be looking at lifetimes, like you said before."

"It's not a matter of time, Peter."

"I know, I know...it's a matter of willingness," my friend finished.

"It's a matter of commitment," Garth corrected him. "Commit to yourself; make your happiness the number one priority in your life, and never delay in choosing it. From now on, don't buy into your victim shit; if you're not feeling good inside, you have the choice to see it as an opportunity to learn something." Xavier paused to look at us. "Or, you can indulge in your victim story. Whichever you choose, just remember that it is your choice. Now, let's take a two hour lunch break!"

✧

When I arrived home, I was surprised to find that Mira had lunch almost prepared. The notes of a pleasant Chopin concerto intermingled with the sizzling of wok-fried veggies cooking on the stove. "How did you know I was coming home now?" I asked, stirring the vegetables absentmindedly, lifting a spoonful high up in the air and dropping them slowly, a bit at a time.

"I don't know; it just felt like you were. It'll be ready in about twenty minutes. If you quit playing with it, that is."

"Sorry." I dropped the wooden spoon dramatically. "That should give me enough time to finish my list of incompletes," I decided, heading for the bedroom.

"I put them on the table," Mira informed me.

"Huh? How did you know…?"

"Me and your teacher are tuned into the same channel." She winked at me, and a rash of goose bumps ran over my arms.

"What channel is that?"

"Channel 69 of course." The thrill of her answer made me feel like a lust-ridden teenager again. I sat down to study my list of unfinished business, realizing that I hadn't looked at it in some time. But much of it I had completed in the course of my days, reminding me of Garth's comment about effortless effort: simply set your intention and let it happen. Except for a few projects that I was still working on, the once intimidating list was now just a few pages of thick black lines. My elation soon gave way, however, to a deeper sense of dread. Now that I had rid myself of the little stuff, the big stuff was beginning to emerge.

"What's the matter?" Mira inquired.

"Nothing."

"Then how come you've got that 'I'm in deep shit now' look on your face?"

"Oh, it's just that, now that I don't have to sweat the little stuff anymore, I have to face my ex and set things straight with her. And then comes the big artillery."

"Your family, right?"

"Right. I tell you Mira, I'm not so sure I can handle Darlene—and we only had four years to build up a good hate. With my family...jeez, we perfected the art of mutual abuse."

"Why do you hate Darlene?"

"I dunno—everyone needs a hobby."

"P.K.," she warned me with her eyes.

"Sorry. I forgot you want blood. I guess I hate her so I don't have to hurt. When she pushed me away, I felt all kinds of things: humiliation, rejection, worthlessness, failure...and I didn't know what to do with them. She took away my dignity, and I felt like a fool—like the whole world was laughing while she castrated me. That's why I hate her: because she's a castrating bitch." I spat the last words out in renewed fury, but it dissipated at the touch of Mira's hand on my arm. "And now I have to forgive her, which means she wins. She got the house, my daughter, most of my friends; my forgiveness was the only thing I could withhold to give me some sense of dignity."

"You don't have to forgive her," Mira reminded me.

"Sure I do."

"Who says?"

"Well...Garth said that I couldn't ever be free if—"

"But you don't want to forgive her. You want to hate her."

"Well," I said reasonably, "nobody wants to hate anybody."

"You do. Admit it."

"I can't. I mean what Garth said—"

"What Garth said, what Garth said..." she mimicked me in a baby voice.

"I say you want to hate her; c'mon and admit it. You'd like to punch her so hard that she'd vaporize. C'mon...c'mon...admit it...you hate her...admit it...." She poked me incessantly in the ribs and stomach, until I exploded with anger.

"Yes I hate her! I'd like to kill the bitch—she ruined my whole life!"

"That's right, and she took your daughter away from you."

"Well no," I corrected her semi-calmly. "Actually, I—hey, don't do that." She was poking me again. "I'm warning you."

"You feel like she took your daughter, your nice house, and the rest of your life, and you want to tear her apart for that. Admit it...c'mon, admit it...." I was beside myself with frustrated rage, partly from the poking, but more from the truth of what she was saying. Screw forgiveness! I wanted that woman to pay! Sitting in the chair while Mira continued to poke and shove me, I let out a long pent-up wail, screaming, "I wish that bitch would...DIE!"

"That's it! Now feel that even more. Just feel all that ugly feeling and enjoy feeling it. Let yourself feel all of it!" I continued with my cursing tantrum, unmindful of the neighbours. I wanted to kill them too! Mira kept urging me on, telling me to feel it more and more, to really get into it. With her coaching, I let my whole body feel the sensation of the hatred until, suddenly, I couldn't feel it any more; it had been replaced with a serene calmness. It wasn't how I usually felt after blowing off steam, or punching a pillow a few hundred times. It was more like the anger had burned itself up in the humour of enjoying it.

"How did you do that?" I asked.

"I didn't—you did."

"But...how?"

"My father used to call it 'celebrating your shit.' You just feel the feeling as completely as possible until it disappears. If you're mad, feel mad; if you're hurt, feel the hurt. But make sure you feel ALL the feeling—not just enough to beat yourself up with." She returned to the stove and continued preparing our lunch. "You don't have to rant and rave like that, but you can if you want. Sometimes it's just not convenient to be a human exhibition. Actually, it can be a lot of fun just to sit quietly somewhere and give yourself over to experiencing the emotion totally. The yelling and screaming is okay, but sometimes it can take you away from what you're really feeling." The phone rang. "I bet you it's Darlene," she said playfully.

"Hello?" I spoke uncertainly.

"Hi, it's me." Darlene's curt voice shot like an electric current through me. "Are you going to pick up Maya tomorrow?"

"Uh, yeah...sure."

"Okay, goodbye." After a hundred or so uncomfortable dealings with me, her conversation was usually abrupt and to the point. Darlene was not about to get drawn into another dispute.

"Hey, wait a minute," I blurted out.

"What—what's the matter?"

"Look..." I took a deep breath to calm myself. "I just wanted to say that...I'm sorry for the way I've been dealing with you. It's just that, well, I don't know—you don't really deserve it."

"That's what I've been telling you. You're the one who left, you know."

"I thought you wanted me to...you told me—"

"I told you to get a life of your own. I didn't tell you to run out on your daughter!" The hell with you, I thought, feeling my blood rise. I looked over at Mira to find her shaking her head and laughing. That broke it for me.

"Yeah, you're right Darlene. I over-reacted. I don't know, it was just stupid pride, I guess. Anyway, I want you to know that I'm sorry, and that I'll treat you with more respect. I don't want to fight anymore." There was a long, possibly suspicious silence at the other end that was finally broken by a subdued, but still curt voice.

"Yeah well, thanks. I have to go. See you tomorrow." I hung up.

"It's a start. I have to admit it does feel better than hating her guts, but it feels like there's a whole lot more in there." Mira was bringing two plates of steaming Chinese food over to the table.

"So?" she responded.

"So, I don't like the feeling," I explained, staring at my lunch.

"No sense asking if the air is good if that's all there is to breath."

"What does that mean?"

"It means if you're feeling something, then feel it."

"But I don't want to hurt anybody with it."

"So don't hurt anybody—who's in charge inside there anyway?" She looked over at me as I continued to stare at my food."You still want lunch, or did you fill up on humble pie?"

"I'm still hungry." I dug in. "After this, maybe we could go into the other room and tune into that channel of yours."

The rain had stopped, at least for awhile, so I decided to take a short walk under the dark grey sky. I thought about the events of the morning session, and how many hurts everyone in the class was carrying inside them. Then I thought of my 'celebrating the shit' with Mira, and I became concerned: was I opening up a Pandora's box? There must have been a half-dozen occasions in class where a student would bring up a problem and I could relate it to something I had been wrestling with for years. It was great to feel it being resolved inside me, and each time it happened I figured that it would be smooth sailing from that point on. But soon another issue would arise and I'd get to see another area of my life in which I felt blocked.

I remembered Garth's words when Peter had asked him point blank, "Hey Garth, does this shit ever end?" His reply was, "Well, from where I'm looking…it never ends. It just gets better, and it gets worse." So what was the point of all this house-cleaning in the subconscious if there was more of the same to look forward to—the same, only worse? Why put myself through all this?

Then I felt it. The thirst that Garth had talked about was filling me with a powerful drive. And I wanted more. It was like wanting to reach out and hug a mountain, or inhale the entire atmosphere! I wanted to embrace life, to experience everything so deeply and so fully that the only words that came from me would be, "Thank you." I ran two blocks to a park that had a small wooded area. Plunging in, I let loose a lustful whoop and cried out, "I WANT TO LIVE! I WANT TO LIVE!" I still didn't know what good working with Garth would do me, but I would keep going with it, as long as I could feel this path beneath my feet. Not the path of survival, or of great achievements, or worldly recognition. It was simply a path of gratitude, and that was more than enough for me. In discovering that this was all I really wanted, I knew the Warrior's Thirst.

THE WARRIOR'S TRUST

"You're thinking too slowly, Peter. At the rate you're going, it could take you years to deal with one single issue in your life."

"Too slow?" Peter reacted to Xavier's statement in surprise. "Man, my problem is that I've got so many thoughts coming in so fast I don't know which one to choose."

"That's not thinking too fast—that's thinking too much. Most people have dialogues going on in their heads; you've got an entire convention. You would be better off using your intuition. It's much more efficient."

"I don't get you; isn't intuition kind of…effeminate?" Cairn suggested.

"Possibly," the teacher conceded. "But it is a pure form of thought. Haven't you noticed how much more quickly things happen when you come from your intuition than when you try to 'figure it all out'?"

"Not really. Mainly because I wasn't using any intuition that I know of; most of the time I was just guessing, you know, making things up. And it works okay in here, but you can't do that in the real world."

"What's so great about the way the real world is working that another way of thinking couldn't help? If you looked at the world's processes, you'd see that many of its failings come from a fractured way of thinking—like the belief that there has to be winners and losers. Only a mind conceived in separation could come up with a belief like that."

"But there *are* winners and losers—it's always been that way."

"Right—and look at how well we've done so far. Plain and simple, that kind of thinking just doesn't work. Rational, logical and analytical thought seems to have only one purpose, as far as I can see, and that's to prove who's right. Do you realize that, without exception, every conflict in the world stems from someone trying to prove they're right? Look at your history books and you'll see that the events leading up to a war followed a logical sequence of steps, with both sides justifying their actions. Even Hitler thought he was right to do what he did. It all seemed perfectly reasonable to him and his generals. These were rational, logical people leading a world full of rational logical people into the irrational, illogical insanity of war. When are we going to learn that a fractured mind can only reinforce separation?"

"What do you mean, 'fractured mind'?" Lyette asked.

"At some point after coming into this world, we started identifying with our bodies—it's been called 'ego/body identification.' This of course came from the choice to believe that we were separate from God. The more we got caught up in believing that we were our bodies, the more we took on distinct personalities. Each personality adopts one of three basic thought patterns. I call them the Collector, the Builder, and the Achiever. Each is a nice way of thinking in its own light but has obvious deficiencies—especially obvious to the other two thought patterns."

"The Builder solves her problem by gathering up as much information as she can possibly find, so that she can build a detailed picture of the problem. Then she carefully builds another detailed picture—this one of all the possible solutions, and the repercussions of each. Builders are very detail-oriented."

"That sounds like me," Vivian put in. She would usually

respond to Garth's questions in a slow, ponderous manner, often weaving a story around her answers, or adding other information that may or may not have been directly related to the subject of discussion. She drove Peter crazy whenever she worked with the teacher.

"I'd say you were a Builder, Vivian," Garth agreed. "Now the Achiever is opposite to this. The Achiever is a very direct-thinking individual. You give an Achiever a problem and she'll give you the quickest, most efficient solution that she can come up with in the twenty or thirty seconds she allots herself. Achievers don't like to waste time—they prefer to cut to the quick."

"That's me!" Cairn announced proudly, "Get things out of the way—fast!"

"That's you all right, Peter," the teacher confirmed. "Then there's the Collector, who's actually an amalgam of the previous two, but not really either. She's an eclectic who likes to take a little from here and a little from there, and produce a whole new picture."

"That's my style," I said, "the best of both worlds."

"Sounds wimpy to me," Cairn argued. "Where would this world be if it wasn't for the achievers? If you waited for those, what d'you call them...Builders...to put food on the table, everybody would starve to death."

"Everybody is starving," Viv countered. "Almost, anyway. And that's because the power is in the hands of the Achievers who go after the quick buck and don't worry about the consequences of their actions."

"At least we do something. I've lost businesses waiting for you people to finish your studies and surveys. Every time the teacher asks you a simple question, you have to give this big long story."

"It's important to give a bit of background," Viv insisted. "There are more sides to me than a one-line answer can show. Life isn't just one dimensional, you know? It has energies influencing it that you have to take into consideration before you understand it. The way you answer leaves so much out that we can never really get to know you."

"At least I get the job done," Peter insisted stubbornly.

"What's that got to do with you as a person? The job isn't worth doing if you don't consider—"

Vivian was cut off by Garth. "As you can see, there are pros and cons to each way of thinking."

"Well, it seems to me," I spoke up smugly, "that the Collector gives you the best of both worlds. It's like we're the balance between the two."

"You're still too slow," Cairn objected.

"You miss a lot of important pieces," Vivian said.

"No I don't. I get the most important stuff in as quick a time as possible. I don't have to read a whole book to pick out what's important—"

"Who's got time to read, man? When you're on the front lines, you can't go running for your books."

"Well, if you prepared a little bit, maybe your life wouldn't be a constant state of emergency," Vivian advised. Before we could bring out the heavy artillery, Garth walked over to the easel and called for our attention.

"As you can see, all three thought patterns are different. They do have one thing in common, however—they all think:

> *Theirs is the right way*

This drew a laugh from all of us, especially the three combatants. "The truth is, if you haven't already guessed, none of them are the best way to think. This is because these forms of thought don't come from you; they come from your personalities—who you think you are. And what's at the very root of these ways of thinking? He wrote the following:

> *Doubt is the epitome of thinking*

Then turned over the paper:

> *All thinking comes from personality*

"Now you each have all three thought forms in you. Naturally one will be the most dominant, while the other two will be suppressed to one extent or another. Like everything else to do with personality, its main function is to enhance the concept of separation. If you end personality, you end thought."

"Why would we want to do that?" Henry wondered.

"Only you can answer that question for yourself. For me, I could not stand all the noises in my head, especially when they kept interfering with my desire to feel good. I found that most of my thoughts were just static that reflected my resistance to feeling loved, or happy."

"Well, why does anyone resist love?"

"I could ask you that, Henry," the teacher responded. Our young classmate thought about it for some ten or twenty seconds before replying.

"I guess because it's too...scary or something."

"Right! Of all human fears, fear of love is the greatest."

"Bullshit!" Peter challenged. I found myself getting tired of his attitude to everything he didn't agree with, but Garth's patience with him seemed limitless.

"Just check out the results: all these other experiences we admit to fearing—death, illness, violence, losing someone—there's a lot more of that going on in the world than people loving each other, or themselves, unconditionally. Remember what I told you: we get whatever we want in this world. If we don't have something, it's because we don't really want it—we want something else more. Results have it that we'd rather die than love."

"That's crazy!"

"True," the teacher agreed with Cairn. "Now, it would be hard enough if we each had only one personality to deal with, but as it happens, there can be up to twenty-nine or thirty major personality complexes inside us. With—"

"What do you mean, complexes?" Marietta interrupted.

"It's sort of like each major personality has a few sub-personalities. Most personalities started being formed around the age of one-and-a-half, whereas the sub-personalities could have come in much later. We'll deal with all this later on. I just wanted to bring up this point: each of your personalities is looking for love. Since each is designed by an ego that can't receive love, the personality will go after what it *thinks* is love. That means that it will chase after attention in the form of conditional acceptance or rejection: love me or hate me, just don't ignore me."

"What, you mean we're all *schizo* or something?"

"Is this a new idea for you, Peter? What I mean is that we're all trying to get love in the way we think will work, but our thinking is fractured and full of doubt. The second principle of the Warrior is, 'Leave no room for doubt in your mind'."

"See?" Cairn nudged me roughly, "I told you it wouldn't be, 'To get ahead you must have a head.'" I ignored him, keeping my eyes on Garth.

"Doubt isn't real, and there's never any justification for entertaining it. Now there will be uncertainty on this path, you can count on it. But you can either see the uncertainty as a chance to jump into fear, and start doubting what is happening. Or you can see it as an opportunity to grow in confidence. When you choose confidence, doubt does not exist. This allows pure thought to emerge."

"What's the difference?" Beverly inquired.

"Pure thought—thought that comes from your essence— is inspired, intuitive, creative, or instinctive. In order to continue your schooling, you'd best learn to rely more on these. They will help you to recognize your personal process, and access the areas of your past where memory will not serve. It's important to understand that your memories are under the ego's domain."

"That sounds all great and everything," loud-mouth Cairn broke in, "but how can you tell when you're using your intuition, and when you're just making things up?"

"Practise, Mr. Cairn; practise and patience. The more you practise using your intuition, the more you'll become attuned to it. The more you attune yourself to it, the more you will trust it. The more you trust it the more you'll get to see the beauty of process in your life. Not only your personal process, but world process as well—and even beyond that."

"What exactly is process?" Vivian asked.

"Process is the interconnectedness of all the manifest energies; nothing happens outside of your process. So the universe can take whatever happens in your life and use it to bring about an experience of Truth. Because with process, all roads lead to love."

"I'm confused. But that ain't news around here," Cairn snorted, looking around the group. You're not kidding, I snarled silently, avoiding his gaze.

"Then you're trying to figure it out—you're thinking," the teacher answered him. "It's a matter of remembering what personal accountability is all about. How else could we affect this world if we were not somehow directly connected to it?"

"Do you mean to tell me you were serious when you told

Kennedy he was responsible for shutting down those companies just so he would lose his clients? That his personal
feelings about money could cause an entire corporation to
collapse?"

"Yup," the teacher replied simply.

"You do realize how insane that sounds, don't you?"

"Only to the small-minded. The Warrior recognizes that
there is nothing beyond him or her. What most of us call
humility is just the ego trying to convince us that we are of too
little stature to influence what occurs around us. It is possible
for Patrick to cause companies to shut down, because Patrick
has that much power—as do you. Now, if you would only
allow it to help you instead of punishing yourselves with it!
This is where your pure mind could inspire you to recognize
that you are an essential part of what you see; that whatever
you choose affects the whole."

"But what about the people in the company who lost their
jobs? They went broke just because P.K. is neurotic about
having money in the bank?"

"They were also choosing along with Patrick. No one
person ever makes a choice alone."

"But why would people want to lose their jobs?"

"Probably for a similar reason that Pat would want to have
money problems," Garth replied calmly, but Cairn remained
unconvinced.

"You mean I could stop all the trouble in the world—the
wars and the sickness—if I *chose* to?"

"Essentially yes, if you went deep enough. Do you
remember what Patrick told us about his increase in clientele
after the work he did in his subconscious, around his parents
and money? And how about your relationship with Jessica
improving after you released that horrible belief about
women?" Garth was referring to something that had taken
place in the class during my three-week absence. "In a month,
you've seen a lot of changes occur in our outer world when
choices were made in our inner ones. And that was dealing
primarily with the subconscious—wait 'til we get deeper."

"Yeah, but a lot of what's happened to the class could be
coincidence. A lot of the changes that happened also
unhappened. Like Kennedy—he got more clients after that
work he did, but he lost them again the next week."

"It could only be a coincidence to who you think you are—your self-concept. As for losing clients, just because you've cleared one part of your subconscious, all your problems won't end. Patrick chose forgiveness, and a positive change took place in his life. If another problem arises, it just means there's more forgiving required of him. We looked at one small place in his subconscious. But see the results for just that little bit of work; imagine if you could find the part of yourself deeper than the subconscious that supports war and suffering. Peter, you haven't even begun to take the kinds of risks you need for your own sake. That's why you're having trouble seeing your influence on the world. First, you have to start remembering who you are." He moved back over to the easel and began to draw circles, much like the ripples in a pool. In the middle circle he made a large G. In the second circle he wrote 'choice,' in the third, 'trauma–pain,' 'guilt–blame' in the fourth, and 'roles, duties, debt payment' in the outer circle.

"This is a simplification of a bigger model I've been working on. It's based on the understanding that we come into this world full of wonderful gifts, talents, and miracles. Our original intention was to give our giftedness to everyone. As an example," he pointed to the middle circle, "this is one of the gifts you had come to give. Then for some reason, you didn't give that gift—you chose not to." He pointed to the second circle, and continued to indicate each of them as he spoke.

"The withholding of the gift was traumatic, forcing us to be aware of the feeling of separation. It causes us, as well as those we love, pain. We look at our family and see the pain they're in and we feel somehow responsible—we take on more feelings of guilt, and feel an obligation to make it better. That's when we assume *roles and duties*, in an attempt to pay off our guilt. We don't even consider giving the gift now, even if we could remember to, because the guilt makes us feel too undeserving. Now, here's the irony of living by roles and duties. Since we're not willing to feel guilty if we can help it, we throw the guilt onto someone else in the form of blame. One minute you're feeling bad because you think you brought pain into your family, and the next minute it's not your fault—it's your mother's or father's. Or the world's! So here we are trying to pay off a debt that we deny is even ours! We're funny critters, aren't we?"

"I'm sorry, but I don't get this," Marlene spoke up. "What you seem to be saying is that I quit loving my mother and brought pain into her life. So I felt guilty about this, and started acting in a certain way to make up for it. But I'm really blaming her inside, thinking that it was she who had stopped loving me—is that what you're saying?"

"Basically, but you're missing an important point. When you withheld love from your mother, you experienced the pain inside first. Then you started to see the pain in her."

"Well, I don't believe that's true. It could have happened that way sometimes, but there were times, I'm sure, when she would just be in a bad mood and take it out on me. I believe in accountability, but she's got to be accountable for what she did too!"

"There are a number of ways we can go with this one, Marlene," the teacher suggested, "but the simplest way I can offer right now is to say that there is no excuse for us to withhold our love. Once we do, we bring on separation. We've done enough processes in the last few weeks which have proven that. And we've also seen that the choice for love—be it through forgiveness, compassion, humour, or whatever—would resolve any problem.

"But you have to see yourself as the starting point. Consider that you saw your mother in pain because she wasn't feeling the love that you had come to give. You felt bad when you saw her hurt, so you acted in such a way as to relieve her pain, and thus your guilt. You misbehaved so that she had to spank you—in that way, you paid off your guilt. Now, you could have become a nice, quiet little girl to make her life easier, or become super helpful, or any number of other ways; you chose this route. But when she spanked you, nothing happened! Nobody felt better, and as a matter of fact, both of you felt worse. At some point the guilt just became too much to bear, so you tried to throw it off yourself, and guess who it landed on—good old Mom. What you never realized is that blaming your mother actually ensures that the guilt stays. Just look at the results: you're still blaming her, and you still feel bad."

"But what about her side of it? She didn't have to spank me!"

"All the more evidence for your rational mind to use in justifying your blame. You have every *right* to blame her—it was her fault. That's what reason will tell you. She spanked you! She was *WRONG!*"

"But she did spank me."

"Okay, so tell me, why did she spank you?"

"Because she was frustrated, probably. This was before she was diagnosed with cancer, and had to stay in bed, but…"

"Hold on," the teacher interrupted. "Frustration usually means that we feel something is being withheld from us, right?"

"I have to think about that," Marlene answered, and then paused to consider. At length she responded. "Well okay, it could mean we're being kept from something or that something isn't happening for us."

"Okay, then what wasn't your mother getting, what wasn't happening for her?"

"She was depressed," Marlene explained. "She was always feeling sick, and no one knew why, and she started to lose hope, I guess."

"Great, then if she had had hope, she would have been okay?"

"Well, she would have still had cancer, but…yeah, she'd be happier."

"Do you think she would have been so inclined to spank you if she had more hope and was happier?"

"I see what you're getting at! But hey, it wasn't my fault she didn't have hope—why'd she take it out on me?"

"Why so defensive?" Garth teased her. "Notice your choice of words—all pointing to the possibility that you do feel responsible."

"So what you're saying is that I could have given her hope, but didn't. So then I made it up to her by being a bad girl to let her take her frustration out on me, and maybe she'd get better then. I wanted her to spank me."

"Sure, being a bad little girl is a classic role. It allows a parent to release their frustrations by getting angry. Problem is, it only lasts as long as the anger, and then the frustration is back, along with a big heaping of guilt to make the parent feel worse. Do you ever screw up big at work?"

"Occasionally," she admitted, "but not often."

"Is it usually around a certain person, by any chance?"

"Always. How did you know?"

"And is this person known around work as an easily-angered or frustrated woman?"

"Exactly—" Marlene's voice became harsh, "—the head nurse on night shifts. She's always acting like she's got a stick up her ass."

"So you're still trying to pay off the debt, aren't you?" Garth's eyes twinkled as he watched Marlene work out what he was saying. It didn't take her long, since she was easily the most brilliant student in the room, but she said nothing more, and he moved on.

"This is getting even more confusing than usual," Cairn complained.

"And depressing," Lyette added. "When do we ever get free of all this? Marlene is still trying to help her mother over an incident that occurred years ago. It all seems so hopeless!"

"What—am I detecting doubt in my Warriors? Have you forgotten the second principle already?" He feigned disappointment. "Trust the process."

"What's there to trust?" Cairn asked. "It's just bad news piled on top of more bad news."

"Trust," Xavier repeated. "The second principle is to remind you to trust that, no matter how many mistakes you make, the Universe will transform them to a higher level of experience. Leave no room in your mind to doubt the power of forgiveness. Leave no room in your mind to doubt your destiny of greatness. And don't doubt that God can change her mind about you. Whenever you find yourself stuck in what looks like a hopeless problem, ask yourself, 'Has God changed his mind about me?' and listen to your heart for the answer. Or 'her mind,' depending on how you view God."

"What if you don't hear anything?" Peter asked. His voice put me on edge.

"Be patient, quiet the inner dialogue—or in Peter's case, the inner world convention—and wait. Your heart doesn't say much, but when it does, it's always on the money, and its voice is as loud as your willingness to hear it. Marlene did the same thing we all did—we continue to play out our roles until we realize a faster, more efficient way to be free of guilt. A way that may not satisfy our logic or our reason, but one that works."

"In case you haven't noticed, the work we've done thus far has primarily been around roles and obligations. Patrick, for the most part we were dealing with your enabler roles— those parts of you that subconsciously believed you had somehow destroyed your family. You're still trying to fix your family. That's why you're in a profession that attracts birds with broken wings. Every time something went wrong, you decided it was up to you to make it better."

"What's wrong with that?" Marlene demanded. "Where would the world be if we had no one to take care of the sick and injured?"

"And where would the enablers be if they didn't have the sick and injured to take care of? My God, they wouldn't have a purpose."

"Are you saying that we're the cause of the sickness in the world?" Marlene was obviously agitated by this line of thinking.

"If you didn't feel that your guilt was real—and incurable, you would no longer see sickness as a hopeless situation that keeps getting worse. If you're driven by some vague feelings of guilt over destroying your family, you will constantly seek opportunities to pay off that guilt. Did you ever notice that feeling of relief—now it may have been really slight—but the feeling that came after you helped relieve someone's pain?"

"Actually," Marlene admitted, "whenever I finish helping someone I feel kind of let down—I even get depressed sometimes."

"Now you do, yes," Garth agreed. "But at first it must have felt somewhat good?"

"At first, yes. But after the novelty wore off, the job got to be more and more of a drag and the only relief I felt was at quitting time."

"Why did you feel good at first?"

"Because I really thought I was helping people—that I was making a difference. Then—"

"You mean, you felt like you were worth something?"

"Yeah, I guess so," Marlene agreed. "But after awhile it just got so overwhelming and the doctors were such jerks—"

"What do you mean?"

"They never appreciated the nurses—"

"—meaning you."

"Not only me, but yeah, I felt like they were walking all over us—"

"—meaning you," the teacher repeated teasingly.

"Okay, okay," Marlene's irritation was beginning to show. "Yeah, they walked all over me and treated me like a cleaning woman—"

"Imagine how the cleaning woman was treated," Xavier broke in again. The student's face was turning red.

"Anyway, I wasn't feeling any reward in my work. If the patients got better, it was the doctors who did it, but if anything went wrong, immediately they'd go on a witch hunt and find a few innocent nurses to burn at the stake. I'm just so fed up with all the hard work and little pay—and no gratitude!"

"Folks," the teacher announced, "you are listening to the voice of an enabler who's in the throes of burnout." A few of us chuckled.

"It's not funny!" Marlene shouted, giving us a start. This was the first day she had really spoken up in the room. "You just try working in my job! Everybody demanding from you and never saying thanks, treating you like a...a...a..."

"Cleaning woman?" Garth guessed, causing a few more chuckles.

"Stop laughing at me! It's not funny." Marlene's eyes watered and her lower lip began to tremble.

"It's never funny to the one who's burnt out, Marlene." Now his voice was quiet and loving. "But don't you notice how familiar these feelings are? Your sacrifice, your feeling of being overwhelmed, anger at the lack of appreciation or respect...and that bad feeling underneath it all...what does it remind you of?"

"My family," Marlene answered, her voice low and weak, as though her energy had been drained away. She kept her gaze on the floor as she spoke. "It's not like they didn't want to be happy; they were just incapable of it. When the cancer really took over my mother, she was in bed all the time, and Dad was no use at all—he'd come home drunk and keep on drinking 'til he passed out. That left me to look after my sister and brothers. I was only eight years old. Someone should've been looking after me, for Chrissake!" I noticed her hands were working on a tissue, tearing it to shreds and letting the tiny pieces fall to her feet. "It was always so dark and gloomy in the house. Just like we were, dark and gloomy all the time."

"So what did you decide to do about it?"

"I don't know," the woman shrugged. "I guess I figured that being a 'bad girl' would only make things worse, so I must have decided that it was up to me to make everything better. So I became the good little girl—bringing Mom her breakfast, and not bothering anyone if I was hurt or lonely or anything. As I got older, I took over running the house. But nothing ever changed, really."

"Nothing ever does," I spoke in a tone of self-pity.

"Spoken like a true victim," Peter commented smugly.

"Aw, give me a break, Cairn!" I snarled.

"What's with you, man?"

"Nothing," I replied churlishly, looking down at my feet.

"Take a valium for Chrissake." The smirk on his face did not leave, and I blew up.

"Aw fuck off! Why don't you just grow up, man. I'm tired of listening to this phoney act of yours! I've been putting up with it for years and it's all a bunch of bullshit. It's always the same old scene: you talk and I listen—and whenever I have something to say, you make fun of it, like you're the only important person on the whole friggin' planet. Well, screw it man, I'm not going to be your doormat anymore!"

"So who asked you to be—you think I need you, man? Shit, Yes Men are a dime a dozen. If you don't want to hang around…çiao—who needs you?"

"Yeah well go f—"

"Will you two stop it?" Vivian demanded. "I hate it when people argue like little kids—why don't you just talk to each other?"

"I've seen this kind of thing happen a lot in group process," Xavier interrupted. "What Marlene's been talking about must have a lot more significance for you than you're aware of. It seems to be bringing up some old pain."

"I'm not in pain—I'm just pissed off," I asserted.

"Anger is a secondary emotion—we use it to control deeper feelings. The pain that Marlene has expressed isn't foreign to any of us, even if the circumstances are. Each of us made similar choices at some time in our lives; we saw pain around us and made it our responsibility to take that pain away." He paused for a few seconds, as if he were considering what to say next. I found myself listening to my breath as the quiet room seemed to get even quieter.

"I want you all to close your eyes. Let your intuition guide you back to a time when you felt that something was somehow wrong with your family. Just look at whatever comes into your mind, and trust it." My mind drifted at first, preferring to stay mainly with my anger at Cairn. Then the music came, again from outside the room. I didn't recognize the piece, but I immediately felt its depth of pathos. Suddenly, what appeared inside me was a picture of my family when I was about six or seven. It was a Sunday afternoon sometime in the summer, and everyone was just hanging around. A dreary mood hung over the house as I wandered from room to room. Nothing on the surface explained the feelings; there was just an all-pervasive sense of…deadness. Each of them was isolated in an enveloping malaise. As the question— why?—played over and over in my mind, I was overcome by a wrenching in my chest, until I almost retched. Why couldn't my family be happy? As the music played on, I heard my classmates crying quietly. A woman's voice sang softly to the tune; the same woman I had heard earlier that day:

> *Whatever happened to the time that never was?*
> *To the sounds of loving voices, and laughter from the*
> *heart.*
> *When the tears that came from eyes were shed*
> *From joy and not from heartbreak*
> *What happened to the ones I loved in a time that*
> *never was?*
>
> *Take me back where my heart flies free;*
> *To a life that breathes constant harmony.*
> *Where people can look with hearts that see*
> *The gift that I am; not what used to be.*
>
> *Whatever happened to the time that never was*
> *To the acts of true caring that loving hands performed?*
> *Where the guiding hands led true*
> *And did not grasp or push away*

Where did you go, and will we meet
In a time that will never be?

As if from a great distance, I heard again the sound of crying. It resonated with the deep sorrow I felt for the loss of my family. Once again I suffered with their blind confusion, helplessly succumbing to the insidious shadow that swallowed up their joy and hope. I couldn't stand it for too long without feeling the urge to rage at God for doing this to us, but I knew the anger was just a cop-out. I wanted to get to the bottom of this. I realized that Garth was talking now, his voice blending in perfectly with the scene I was witnessing, and the soft sweet music.

"Now look at what they're missing. What is it they really need to heal their pain?" The words 'sense of purpose' popped into my head. I looked at my parents and saw that they had lost theirs altogether, and that my brothers and sisters were in the process of abandoning their purpose. "What they're missing is the gift you had come to give them. This gift would have mended their wounds, can you see that? You just forgot. You made the mistake of forgetting that you were—and are— gifted, and that if you had let your gift shine, your family could have remembered the same gift in themselves! If you had lit the candle of your giftedness, it would have shone enough light for them to see theirs. You just forgot, that's all—it was a mistake. You didn't do anything wrong, like you choose to think you did. And guess what," Garth's voice was full of a soft sweetness. "It's not too late. Where you are right now, and with what is happening inside you…you can choose that gift now! Just want to." Okay, I said, with sincerity and desperation, I want to give my gift of purpose. I need to give my gift of purpose! Even as I said the words though, I seriously doubted that anything would change. On that cue, Garth resumed.

"Leave no room for doubt in your mind. Don't give space to your cynical, despairing, critical, or any of your other doubt-filled personalities. Use the Warrior's Trust, and want to give your gift. All your life you've tried to undo the mistakes and sins of your past. But you never did anything wrong; you just judged yourself harshly, and assigned yourself a role to pay off the guilt."

"So how have you done so far? Is the debt finally paid off? Have your wrongs been righted? How many years of this before you'll see that it's not working? Patrick, are you going to burn out completely at work before you see that it hasn't saved your family? And Peter, how many more years will you spend out there in the wastelands of independence, hiding your needs because you thought they had destroyed your family? And Vivian, how many more years in your dependent roles? Getting sick or plagued with bad luck, hoping that your parents will see that you're paying for all the awful things you did? It doesn't have to be this way—you don't have to pay for mistakes—you're found innocent, and all your debts are hereby declared null and void. You may now reclaim your gifts."

I wished it were that easy. It was as if something inside me was working against my own best interests. Each time I gathered up the energy to choose the gift, the rug was yanked out from under me, and I began free-falling in a tunnel of despair. As soon as that happened I felt myself fighting off the dark sensation.

"Resist nothing," Garth reminded us. I let myself fall. The despair intensified and the darkness grew, but strangely enough my mind became quieter, and steady resolve unfolded in me. The pain and the darkness were still there, but I was more absorbed by my love for Garth. The love expanded to enfold more of the people in my life: Maya, my angel of a daughter. And Mira. More and more faces appeared in the blackness, each one reflecting a recognition of true affection and appreciation. Not because of who they were, but...well...just because it felt so natural to love them. "Whatever you're experiencing, don't forget your gift. It has always been inside you, but you forgot when you stopped giving it." Following the teacher's guidance, I called out in my silent thirst and was answered by a dim glow that seemed to encompass me. I reached forth with my will, to the centre of the light.

Wandering through the house, I peaked in again on every member of my family, just as I had done earlier. On the outside they all looked to be in the same state as before—not really doing anything of importance. But this time when I looked in their eyes I saw something different. It was as if it was all right for them to be where they were, doing whatever they were doing. As I watched them, I perceived a peacefulness around them. Although their lives were not going anywhere at that moment, as far as I could see, they were simply glad to be there—alive, and feeling good for no particular reason. This, I realized, is the gift of purpose. It was what I had always wanted for them.

"I'm sorry, I'm sorry, I'm sorry..." Once again, Peter's voice pulled me out of my reverie, but this time he sounded different. I looked over to see his large frame shaking heavily as his tightly closed eyes released a flow of tears, and his hands ripped at the tissue he was holding. Whatever was going on inside of him had to be pretty wild. His shirt was soaked in sweat.

"How are you doing, Peter?" Xavier inquired gently.

"It hurts so much!" Peter wailed. "Everybody's fighting with each other, and my father's upstairs with cancer eating his bones, and, and, ...and everybody is in so much pain! And they're all scared...and I can't do anything for any of them!"

"And what is it they're crying for? What gift do you have?"

"Fuck gifts, man—this is real! This happened! They were hurting and I ran out on them. I was the only one working, and I left them to starve! My whole family went down the toilet and I just let them!" His crying turned into a long plaintive wail that pushed me deeper into my own emotions. I'd known him almost all my life, and I had never seen as much as a tear. The music stopped, and Garth moved closer to the big man.

"So you ran out on your family," Garth continued after the crying had subsided to an occasional whimper. "What were you feeling inside that caused you to leave?"

"I couldn't stand to watch it. I just didn't want to see!"

"And what did watching it bring up in you?" Garth persisted. "What exactly made you run?"

"I...don't...know!"

"Go in there and feel it."

"I tell you, I can't feel anything. Okay, so maybe I'm a little scared of all the responsibility they're putting on me, but that's 'cause I'm too young for it!"

"Okay, and what was it that caused you to take on the responsibility in the first place?"

"Well, somebody had to! I was the oldest boy, and Dad

was sick—hell, I had been doing it since I was seven. But when things got really bad, it just seemed like too much—like I was getting old too fast."

"And what were you feeling when things got really bad? Check out your feelings when you look at the scene just before you left."

"Give me a break, Garth," Cairn breathed tiredly. "I tell you I don't know—I'm not good with feelings."

"Give you a BREAK?" Garth yelled suddenly, "I'm trying to save your LIFE—how's that for a break? Now, what were you feeling?" Peter was as stunned as the rest of us. He became very still, closing his eyes again. At length he spoke, and there was humility in his voice.

"We're sitting around the kitchen table and everyone is telling me what the doctor told my mother, about Dad having maybe two more months. Then Mum up and announces that the medical bills ate up all Dad's life insurance. Plus we're in debt up to our teeth and mortgaged to the hilt. And all of a sudden, everyone turns to ME, like I'm supposed to come up with some great miracle or something…"

"And how did that make you feel?" the teacher asked, and there was a look of anticipation or excitement in his eyes.

"Weak," Peter answered simply. Then, "I felt like it was all too much for me, and that I wasn't strong enough for the…the…whatever waited up ahead. I hate feeling weak."

"So what did you decide to do?"

"Like I said, I cut out."

"And what happened to that feeling of weakness?"

"I dunno. I guess I made sure I'd never feel it again."

"So what would you do if that feeling did come up?" Xavier wondered.

"It never has yet—not that I know of," Peter replied, almost proudly.

"No?" the teacher pulled back his head in surprise. "That's funny, I could have sworn that I saw it coming up between you and Patrick a few minutes ago."

"Aw, we do that all the time."

"I'm sure you do—every time you start feeling that weakness and he starts to feel like he's done something wrong—that he's destroyed something." The teacher looked at me and smiled that knowing smile.

"I wasn't feeling like that," I objected.

"Me neither," Peter chimed in.

"Of course not—not on a conscious level, anyway. Do you think your ego would clue you in? It was your anger that tipped your hand. You thought you were just fed up with each other, right? Just like all the other times. But, I'll let you in on a little secret." He walked over to the easel and printed:

We are never angry for

Next page:

the reasons that we think.

"Your anger was a way of controlling what was happening inside you, to stop you from feeling the pain and guilt that was coming up. It was happening with all of us, and each of us probably tried to control it in our own way. Luckily, we had Marlene here to give us an opening. How are you doing now, Marlene?"

"Fine." The woman smiled warmly, tears still in her eyes. "I feel like there's hope for all of us now. Thank you, Garth."

"You're welcome." They looked at each other for a long time, before Garth turned back to the rest of us. His eyes were moist. "If one person takes a risk in this group, and goes into his or her feelings, the rest of us will soon follow. Now this 'gift process' has been building all morning and afternoon; I could see it in your faces and body language."

"How come we didn't notice?" I wondered.

"Because you didn't want to feel shitty, probably. We have a knee-jerk response to guilt and pain: we don't know how to be free of them, so we set up subconscious defenses to make sure we don't feel them."

"So if we feel pissed off or lousy, that's good, right?" Cairn inquired innocently, and I remembered why I loved that man.

"It means that some old hurt is surfacing in your consciousness to be healed. Whenever pain comes up in you, forgiveness and love can't be far behind. It's come up many times in many of your relationships—it's just that you and Patrick are so close it's more apparent. It's closer to home. But whenever, absolutely every time, you and Patrick got together, there was an opportunity to heal that pain and receive a gift back. The trouble is that instead you would each go into your roles: Patrick would become the good ol' enabler—ever-attentive and polite—and you would become the die-hard independent. Never expose your weakness…never show your need. Instead of having a true partnership where you could stand naked and defenseless before each other, you had what's called a cautious friendship, protected by your roles."

"Okay, so say we did bring up this old pain, like I'm feeling right now—what the hell do we do with it? How can I ever feel okay about running out on my family?"

"We all ran out on our families," Vivian commented. "It was a mistake, like the teacher said."

"Yeah?" Peter sneered coldly. "Well, I don't think that your mistake put your brother in jail, or turned your sister into a hooker."

"I don't have a brother," Viv shot back.

"This is just more pain coming up," Garth cut in, looking at Vivian to remind her that there was something in this for her, too.

"What the hell am I supposed to do with it?" Peter exploded, jumping up from his chair and towering over the seated teacher. "There are some things in this world that you have to live with! What's done is done, and no amount of your goddamn forgiveness is going to change that."

"Is this what's kept you from having the kind of success you want in your life?" Garth asked, looking directly into my friend's eyes.

"What?" Peter demanded.

"Have you been letting your guilt about abandoning your family stop you from being happy?" At this question, Peter's shoulders dropped and he returned to his chair.

"What're you talking about—I do all right."

"Yes, but can you enjoy it, knowing that you had to abandon your family to get this far?" Peter did not answer, but stared back at the teacher like a man whose whole life's act had just been exposed and busted. "You see, Peter, the trouble with being caught in an independent role is that you can't really enjoy your successes, because it means that you would have to feel."

"So what's the way out of it?" my friend asked hollowly.

"Receive the gift," was the simple reply. "What was it that your family was lacking at the time you left them?"

"Self-confidence. They were all looking to me, because they didn't have faith in themselves, that they could do it."

"Great!" the teacher acknowledged his answer enthusiastically, "And do you see how you never got that for yourself?"

"Yeah! I could never trust myself, because I always thought that I would cut out if the going got tough."

"Right! Now where did you expect the confidence to come from—God or yourself?"

"I never was much on God, so I guess I expected me to come up with it. And when I couldn't feel it, that's when I started to feel weak, and that's when I ran."

"Okay, so now go back to that scene in your mind—when you were sitting around the table with your family—"

"I don't want to."

"Because…?"

"Because I don't want to feel that weakness. I don't believe there's a God who can heal it, and even if there were a God, what's done is done—I don't believe that you can change the past."

"Didn't you tell me you have a daughter, Peter?"

"Yeah, Crystal."

"Is that how you want Crystal to live her life—chained to the past? Living a life of regret over some innocent mistake, just like her dear old dad?"

"That's a low blow," Cairn said quietly.

"You can show her a better way. You can show her—not to mention a thousand or so others—that we don't have to pay forever for our mistakes. We can forgive ourselves and move on. Or you can teach her that she's fated to be a victim of some blind error that she won't even remember, and that she has to live the rest of her life in guilt, bitterness and fear."

"It's different for her, man. She's not in the same situation—she's got it a whole lot easier than I ever did."

"You said you felt responsible for everything that happened in your family, didn't you?"

"Well…yeah, in a way," Peter admitted.

"And don't you think your daughter feels that she had something to do with you and your wife breaking up?"

"I know she does, and I keep telling her it wasn't her fault—me and Darlah just couldn't get along."

"But Crystal keeps feeling guilty. I'm telling you that your father's cancer wasn't your fault, and that it wasn't your fault that you felt weak and had to leave—do you feel forgiven? Then how can you expect her to—she's waiting for you to show her how."

"But some things are different!" By the sound in Peter's voice, it was obvious that his love for his daughter was melting his argument.

"Just play along with me on this, okay? My rules. I'm not even going to change the scene at all—everything happened just the way you described it, okay?"

"Sure," Pete agreed, "so we're all sitting around the table, and they're giving me all this bad news. Now what?"

"Now," the teacher took over, "feel that weakness come over you—look into their eyes and notice their look of hunger and expectation; how's that?"

"It makes me feel like I'm supposed to be a superman—it's like they don't even care about all the things I've done. They want to know what I'm going to do for them and all I feel is empty and weak—like I'm not enough anymore."

"Okay, now imagine that you're feeling really confident. Pretend you're the chairman of this corporation and your family are the board members. What would you say to them?"

"Now that I can relate to," Peter announced firmly. "I'd just look at them and tell them to get off their asses—that we're a team, not a one-man show. And if they kept on whining like they did that night, I'd tell them to quit feeling sorry for themselves, and act like responsible individuals. I've had to give that speech a lot in my life."

"So what if they tell you they just haven't got what it takes? Quickly, Peter. Don't think about it—what would you say?"

"I'd tell them that we've all got it; that if they can see it in me then it's in them too. They've just got to," his voice began to falter, "I dunno...find it, or ask for it or something.... See, this is where it all fell apart—even in my life now. I've had board meetings like that and I don't know what to tell my people when it gets to that stage."

"Funny how that same scene keeps coming up in your life, isn't it? I bet it came up in your last relationship, too. When your wife was doubting herself, or wanting you to carry her."

"That's when I cut out, man. I couldn't handle Darlah latching onto me like that. It really pissed me off, and I didn't know how to talk about it."

"Okay, now let's go back to that scene at your house; this time though, see yourself asking for help. Just imagine that you did that—what would it look like?"

"Well, I didn't believe in God, so...I see myself feeling that weakness, and feeling like I have no one to turn to. So I just keep sitting there...and then I just get desperate, and...something jumps out of me—out of my chest—like some kind of prayer. Only I don't know who to pray to, so I just leave it open. You know, something like, 'I don't know if there's anyone or anything out there, but I could really use a break right about now'."

"Great, great! Now say an idea pops into your head at that point—what would that be? Quick, don't think."

"Leave. I get the feeling to leave, so when everybody's asleep that night, I pack up and walk. Just like I really did."

"Okay, but now what are you feeling when you leave?"

"I'm really hurting. I know my family will never under-stand, and I don't think I'll ever see them again. So I feel this big pain in my chest."

"And what about the guilt?" Xavier asked.

"Oh it's there all right. But I seem to feel different in some way. I feel really bad about leaving them, but something tells me it's for the best. Is that a cop-out?"

"What does your heart tell you?"

"I dunno, I can't hear it. But there is this warm energy in my chest right now. It makes me see that I did what was best for everyone—but there's this voice in my head that's telling me I'm bullshitting, that what I did was wrong."

"Which feels truer?"

"The voice in my head is more convincing."

"That's not what I asked," Xavier pushed on. "I asked which feels truer?"

"That heat in my chest—but I still keep thinking that I'm letting myself off the hook. It's like I'm being torn in two."

"Conflict will do that to you; it happens when your heart is calling you one way and your head another. Why don't we check it out—what's the result of having listened to your head all these years?"

"Well, basically it's been horse shit."

"Now, let's look at that scene through your heart's eyes,

but notice we don't change anything that happened. You're packing up and leaving, and of course your mind is attacking you full force. But listen to the warmth in your chest—what would it say if you put that warmth into words?"

"That it's okay." Peter's voice was soft, with a tinge of wonder. "That it's what's best for everybody. It'll give them the chance to find their own strength, instead of looking outside for it."

"So how does that feel? Does it feel true?"

"Yeah!" my friend declared enthusiastically. But then his shoulders dropped again. "But that isn't what happened— they didn't find it inside themselves; they just got lost."

"Just listen to that warmth in you—what does it tell you?"

"It's saying not to worry. Easy for it!"

"Don't brush off anything that voice says. Worrying about your family didn't help them, and it certainly didn't improve your life. Worrying about someone just tells them that, because you didn't make it, they won't either. And what a coincidence, you held that thought in your mind and look how they turned out!"

"You mean, just because I listened to the wrong voice, my whole family got screwed up? So if I had listened to my heart, they would have turned out great? Now I feel even worse."

"That's because you're listening to the wrong voice again. Feel that warmth inside you and tell me—"

"I've lost it." Peter opened his eyes and shook his head sadly.

"It's a good thing it never loses you," Garth said cheerfully. "Just imagine—just for fun—that you did listen to your heart. How would you view what happened in your family?"

"Okay, just to humour you...I'd say they chose their own paths to walk on."

"So your heart wasn't lying to you when you left?"

"Yeah, it's possible," Peter conceded.

"What would your heart say about the paths they chose?"

"I guess, not to worry, that they have the strength within them and that help is always there for them."

"Now, how does it feel for you to beat yourself up with guilt?"

"It feels horrible."

"And what feeling do you get when you cheer them on,

with faith that they'll make it, no matter what?"

"It's really great! Just thinking about it gives me this big, expanded sensation in my chest! But—"

"Keep your butt out of this," Garth advised in a southern drawl.

"This is your choice: the voice of your ego with all its guilt, blame, and victim guano, or the voice of your heart, with all its love, forgiveness, compassion—and hope. It takes nothing at all to listen to the first—you've had years of practise being guilt-ridden and full of fear. But to listen to your heart—now that's the essence of the Warrior's training! It takes extraordinary patience, perseverance in the face of uncertainty and confusion, and the humility to admit that you don't know."

"Sounds great! But how does it change the way my family is doing? I mean, I can hold all the confidence in the world for my brother, but it won't get him out of jail. What real *good* does it do to listen to your heart?"

"C'mon Pete," I said good naturedly, "Let's get real here— what's it done for you to follow the other voice. Maybe it won't get Jimmy out of jail, but it'll make your life easier and it'll give your brother something when he gets out. It'll give him his big brother back."

"Exactly," Garth agreed, "and who knows what can happen. A Warrior recognizes that what happens outside is merely a reflection of what's going on inside, that events are important only as a mirror. So if you don't like what you see, it's pointless to try and change the mirror. Change the thing that's being reflected."

"We did really good work today—it felt great to see the support you gave each other and the trust you put into the process." He acknowledged each of us with appreciative eyes. When he looked at me, I felt like I had been blasted by a small bolt of lightening. I suddenly felt big.

The teacher walked up to the easel, and wrote these words:

INDEPENDENT—MAVERICK

HELPER—ENABLER

DEPENDENT—NEEDY

"Now, here's your homework. These are the three major

roles in our subconscious. All other roles are variations of one
of these. For instance, you could be a 'goody-goody' or a
superman, and they would be aspects of the Helper. Or you
could be the trouble-maker or the lonesome cowboy, and
these would come from an Independent role. I want you to
take stock of all your roles and duties—all the social obligations you would feel too guilty to let go of, and then put down
beside each one the person whose forgiveness you're trying
to win, or who you're trying to fix."

"What do you mean, 'fix'?"

"You're trying to fix someone when making them happy
becomes your job."

"How can you tell the difference between a role and a true
action?" Beverly asked.

"Good question, Bev. It's really simple—when you're in
a role, you can't receive anything. Your actions aren't fulfilling
to you, but you'd still feel really bad if you stopped. If you're
giving from the heart, you're filled just by the giving, and
you're not attached to the results. In a role, the results are very
important, because they are intended to assuage the guilt and
pay off the old debt."

"So beside the names, I want you to name the debt you're
trying to pay off. We'll meet back here tomorrow morning at
nine o'clock."

"Nine?!" most of us cried out. It was past eleven-thirty, and
we were very tired.

"Okay, okay," the teacher conceded. "Jeez, I must be
getting soft in my old age; make it nine-thirty."

As I took the short walk home, I thought about Garth. I
wondered what had got him into this kind of work, and what
kind of person he was. I had often read about great leaders,
masters and teachers, and I had always believed these people
were different: born under special circumstances, specially
schooled, trained to go into the world and save the rest of us
lesser beings. But as I watched Garth work, I was taken by
how normal he was—almost, as he had said, an old friend

returning a favour. But what could I have ever done for him, and when?

Then I thought about the work he had done with Peter, and the look on my friend's face when it was over. It wasn't Peter's smile nor his relaxed composure; there was a new depth in his eyes, like in Garth's. Then I realized what set Garth apart from most people I knew. It was simply that he had chosen to look at the world through the eyes of forgiveness. He listened to his heart and trusted its voice.

"You just walked past your house," I heard from behind. On turning to see Garth, I felt suddenly nervous and awkward.

"This is a nice neighbourhood to go walking in at night. Especially good for grounding out after a session like today's." I mumbled some sort of affirmative reply. We walked for a while in silence as I endeavoured to master my discomfort, once more going into the centre of the most uncomfortable feeling, and letting it melt away.

"Have you figured it out yet, what you're doing in this course?"

"Not really," I responded huskily.

"Good," he said. "I've been doing this kind of training for fifteen years now, and I still haven't figured it out. I think I even stopped trying."

"You mean you don't know what you're doing?"

"Most of the time, no. I just wait for instructions and then follow them."

"Instructions—you mean from your intuition?"

"Partially, I guess. To be more accurate, I wait for heaven to pass down the orders. It keeps me on my toes, seeing as how I'm usually informed one step at a time."

"Is that how you decide what to teach us?"

"That, and watching the group process. Today there was a heavy, burdened feeling among you, and a lot of people were really caught up in their roles, so I went with that."

"But, isn't there some kind of program you follow?"

"I tried that once, but it became apparent all too quickly that people's lives had their own programs. How could I fit what had happened to Peter and Marlene into a set course? They were ready to take the dive, and clear up a major block for the whole group, so that's what we did."

"I really don't get that," I declared, feeling more comfortable as we walked. "Actually, there are two things that I don't get—"

"More like two million," the teacher interjected.

"Yeah, well anyway, the two that are bugging me right now are—how can what someone else did do me any good? I know it works, but I just can't grasp how it works. My upbringing and theirs are completely different. And the second thing you said was that every time Peter and I get pissed off with each other, it's because of some old pain coming up. Sometimes he just bugs me because he's being Peter, and I get tired of it."

"Well, to answer the first one, any time we choose forgiveness, we choose for all of us. You saw that we're all connected, and even if you can't experience right now what you felt then, something inside you holds the memory; something inside you knows that it's true."

"Then, why should I make myself the priority if everyone else is just as important?"

"You're trying to use reason to understand a paradox, Patrick. You *are* us. Look—why do you think I do this kind of work?"

"To help people like me?"

"Wrong. I do it because it's the best thing I can do for myself. Because I get my orders from on high, and those orders are always concerned with my best interests. When they tell me to pursue some other course of action, that's what I'll do, by the Grace. I'm not out to help anybody, or try to make the world a better place—that would be stupid. Not that I didn't try that when I was young and foolish. I had those ideals; you know, save the world! Help bring world peace! But I realized that I was trying to change the outside in order to delay looking inside, all the while hoping that my changing out there would somehow change in here without me having to deal with in here. No, I'm teaching you because it's true for me. I make myself the priority by always doing what's true for me, and since we're all the same, my acts benefit all of us equally."

"I know it's benefiting me, that's for sure," I told him. After a few steps I added, "Well, I know it's doing something for me, anyway." We both laughed at this, and for a brief moment it did feel like we were two old friends.

"We've only begun, Patrick. Between me and your new sweetheart, you're in for more than a few surprises. You think family obligations are something, wait'll we get deeper into Vision and Mastery. You still haven't dealt with power struggle yet, which brings us to your second question."

"Yeah, I guess it does," I declared uncertainly. "What was my second question?"

"You said you couldn't see how being angry with Peter meant old pain was coming up."

"Oh yeah! Sometimes accountability makes perfect sense to me, and then Cairn goes into one of his numbers, and I don't see what it's got to do with me at all. Couldn't it be a personality thing? The guy can be a real dork sometimes and even though he's my best friend, sometimes I'm not able to handle it."

"Only because there's a feeling of discomfort inside you that's being aggravated by his behaviour. It happens in all relationships. I have a feeling that it's really going to come up with Mira—and pretty soon too! But a great deal of time and pain can be saved if you learn a few vital points. First of all, you have to see that everything happens within some form of relationship. So if you get hurt in one relationship, another one has the potential to heal the hurt. You think that because something went wrong with your Mom, and now she's dead, you can never be free of what happened. What you don't see is that it wasn't that person in that body which was so important—I mean, it doesn't matter that it was your Mom. What matters is the level of intimacy you had with her. As a child you were at such a deep, open space, that everyone meant so much to you. It follows that when something went wrong, it was of great significance. Since you closed up more and more after each hurt, the deeper levels of intimacy became less available to you. Ever notice that when you get hurt by a woman who you really cared for, and you don't release the hurt completely, it's hard to imagine loving someone that deeply again? It's the same thing with your family—things went wrong when you were at such a strong feeling place, that nowadays, you can't really relate to what actually happened because you're not willing to go to the place inside where the hurt occurred.

"Wait a minute," I interrupted, "I want to make sure I get

this. You're saying that every time I got hurt, if I didn't get over it, I'd just leave it and decide not to go near it again, right? So I just made myself forget that it ever happened, but to do that, I have to deny that those feelings exist inside me. So whenever I get real close to someone, I get close to those feelings, too. Like, if I start feeling as much love for Mira as I did for my mother when I was a baby, then I might re-experience those old traumas."

"Basically. And those feelings and that level of intimacy *will* come up between you and Mira. Or with anyone else you get close to—if you have the courage to face the feelings, that is. A little known fact in this world concerning conflict is that both parties in the conflict are feeling the exact same feelings inside, but reacting to them in opposite ways. In other words, both you and Peter were feeling some old pain that came from thinking you had somehow destroyed your families. When that feeling began to emerge into your awareness, you decided to suppress it with your anger. The anger directed you away from the pain by making the problem external. As long as Peter was the problem, you didn't have to address your own inner process. We're never upset for the reasons we think, because anger is used to control the emotions, and distract us from the real issue by involving us in a fight. Of course, you and Peter both have had a lot of practise with your ex-wives."

"Not me, I never argued. Peter and Darlah used to go at it like cats and dogs."

"Knowing you," Garth nudged me, "you probably withdrew from your wife, right?"

"I just didn't see the point in arguing, so I'd go for a walk, or not say anything for a while—"

"Like a week or two. You just used the most vicious form of anger, Pat—you withdrew. Either way, everyone was trying to control the painful feelings that were the real issue. Man, are we going to have fun in the next few months!" Garth chuckled and rubbed his hands enthusiastically, and I realized that he truly loved his work, with a kind of youthful enthusiasm I could not recall ever having felt in my own work as a psychologist.

We walked in silence as I contemplated what he had just told me. The fights I used to have with Darlene were more like cold wars, most of the time. I realized how completely ludicrous they were and how much time I had wasted trying to get her to change so I would feel better. Why couldn't I just let go of my position, and spend the time in sharing love and fun with my family? If Darlene did something that bothered or hurt me, I would pout until she came around to seeing things the right way—my way. But as time went on, waiting for the apology became an endurance test, as it took longer and longer to come, grudgingly, from her. And when she did apologize, I felt unaccountably worse—the days of cold silence and bitterness were too high a price to pay for my victory.

"Yup," Garth spoke once again, as though he had heard my thoughts. "You can't feel very good in a relationship when you spend most of it trying to control your partner. It would help you to know that the world is one big classroom, and its only lesson is to teach you how to hear and respond to the call to come home. Every conflict, every situation, every relationship provides you with that chance."

"Well that really pisses me off! How are we supposed to know that? I've been in and out of a dozen relationships, and I didn't have a clue about their real purpose, or the opportunities they held. What's the use of all this if you don't know what it's for? Here you are telling me now what I could have done in my last relationship when it would have been a hell of a lot more helpful back then, when I needed it! Everything seems to come after the fact; I spent the first thirty years of my life screwing it up, and now it looks like I'll have to spend the next thirty years undoing what I did in the first thirty. Why wasn't I told anything? What's the use of this world being one big classroom, if nobody knows? It's not—"

"Fair?" Xavier guessed.

"Well, yeah."

"It's a funny thing about time, you know, Patrick? Because we think of it in a certain way—you know, linearly, from past to future—we get caught in all kinds of traps. All our mistakes, failures and losses are locked away in the unreachable past, as though what's done is carved in the stone of our guilt. And the future is as much out of reach. We stagger toward it with fear, anxiety, and a constantly fading hope, as the energy of our youth becomes more and more depleted with each passing day. Our options are diminished and the light of our promise gets dimmer. But what if our perception of time was just another trick of the ego?"

"What do you mean—what other way could time be?"

"What if we could actually change the past, by something we do right now? And if by changing our past, our future would be transformed as well?"

"I can't imagine that. I think it would be more confusing than it already is."

"I met this woman from Jamaica who had an amazing story. Ria had been abandoned by both her parents, and left on her paternal grandmother's doorstep. As it turned out, the grandmother was quite poor, and really resented having another mouth to feed. So the little girl grew up with a woman who loathed her very existence, and wouldn't let her forget whose fault it was that they were so poor."

"Anyway, the years went by and the little girl endured the abuse until she was old enough to get away from her grandmother. A short time later, the old woman got sick and unable to care for herself, so all the relatives got together to discuss what to do about her. Since none of them wanted to take care of her—she being such a pain in the ass with her incessant complaining—a huge family feud raged for weeks as they passed her around from one household to the next, arguing bitterly about whose responsibility she was. Through some bizarre, twisted logic, the sons and daughters concluded that it was the abandoned granddaughter's duty to take care of her."

"At first, the eighteen-year-old woman would have nothing to do with that idea, but after a good deal of pressure, she relented. A few weeks after she had taken the woman under her care, I happened to meet her while I was vacationing in Jamaica. A good thing too, because Ria was seriously considering killing her Grandmother—she was at her wits' end. I spent some time with Ria, and she came around to deciding to try a different approach. For the next two years, she served the old woman with as much love and forgiveness as she could let in. It wasn't easy at first, but somehow she knew that there was no other way."

"After two years, the woman died, but do you know what she told me before she died? She recounted to me her whole life, from childhood right through her time with Ria, and all she could express was how rich her entire life had been. She kept using that word, 'rich,' over and over. Ria was listening too, and was shocked; it was a far different story than the one she had grown up listening to. But those few years of service had changed the grandmother's entire life—had literally transformed her past. Not only that, but Ria realized that as she thought about her life with the old woman, all the pain and poverty were gone and what remained was only the love. At the funeral, the one who had the most cause to hate, grieved the passing of a loved one most deeply."

"That's pretty amazing," I admitted. "If I was Ria, I probably would have given old grandma the finger."

"My wife Ria is a pretty amazing woman." Garth smiled at my surprise. "But she did what any human being can do: she chose love over revenge." Suddenly, we both stopped and faced each other. He held my eyes with his.

"Do you really think there is something that love cannot do? All the time you feel you've wasted, and then compound the waste with regret—do you think love can't work one of its miracles, and transform that regret into gratitude, and the waste into valuable lessons?"

"Well," I said, shifting my eyes uncomfortably, "I'd like to believe it. I just haven't seen much to prove that it can do what you say. Love has been a pretty elusive commodity in my life. Even what I used to call love, you've pretty well shown me it's mostly been some passing emotion. So now, I tell you Garth, I don't know if I'd know real love if it hit me on the head!"

"But I really think you've experienced a love that's powerful enough even to transform time—so that's why I'm at your doorstep like some kind of spiritual beggar. I've got my little bit of willingness, my little bit of determination, and a very faint thirst which I've only just recently found in me. I have no idea what a Warrior is, and I don't even know if I want to be one. All I know is that when I look at you, I see a possibility…and that's all I know." He looked deep into my eyes, and I felt an overwhelming sense of timelessness, as though we had played this ritual out before. Maybe the place was different…maybe even the bodies were different, but the recognition and knowing were still the same.

"Patrick," he said finally, putting his arm around my shoulder and leading me back toward my house and my waiting Mira, "this looks like the continuation of a beautiful friendship." His Bogart imitation was only slightly better than average.

APPENDIX

don't second themselves to the world.

13. What you see is what you choose to see. Often you are not aware of the place within where the choice is originating.

14. In the subconscious mind, whatever happened in the past is *still* happening now. The outside players may change but the dynamics of the conflict remain the same.

15. If you can't trust your own inner voice, what can you trust?

16. There is only one commitment—commitment to yourself.

17. Everyone benefits from the fulfillment of your true goals and purpose, otherwise your goals and purpose are simply not true.

18. The subconscious mind holds the records of each time we chose not to see the interconnectedness of humanity.

19. Warrior's Resolve: I am the priority in my life. I will not succumb to the temptation to sacrifice or indulge, for whatever I sacrifice to, or indulge in becomes more important than me.

20. Grace carries you to your purpose without effort or demand.

21. Warrior's Discipline: I am willing and determined to *allow* the grace to carry me.

22. The Warrior's Discipline is the practice of effortless effort.

23. Results = Intentions

24. Sacrificers are driven to sabotage their lives by the perception that what lies ahead is just more sacrifice—so they "blow up" what's in front of them.

25. You will feel rejected when you want something from someone, and they don't give it to you. It is actually you who does the rejecting.

26. True giving carries no fear of rejection.

27. If there is love, nothing matters. If there is no love, nothing matters.

28. Work without joy is an insult to all that is true in life.

29. The concept of earning comes from the feeling that you are unworthy to receive.

30. ALL relationships mirror your inner process.

31. We enter the family of our choice with the original intention to serve unconditionally.

32. Only in true giving can one truly receive.

33. Procrastinators make time their boss.

34. If you don't have something in your life, it's because you don't really want it—you want something else more. You don't have to like what you want—you just have to want it.

35. A Warrior is greater than any emotion or feeling.

36. Awareness shrinks what is not true and allows what is true to grow.

37. Habits and patterns are largely geared toward avoiding discomfort or making a discomfort bearable by making it familiar.

38. Determination grows as you realize you are worth the constant effort. That realization comes from your willingness. You just have to want it.

39. You chase the things of the world to prove your right to happiness. If you own happiness as your birthright, the things of the world will chase you.

40. You can not measure your "spiritual progress" by phenomena.

41. Every choice you make affects the whole—it's all interconnected.

42. So many beautiful experiences are lost in the attempt to prove their validity.

43. ALL pain comes from attachment.

44. Be willing to face your pain and choose forgiveness, rather than seeking revenge on the one who you think caused the pain.

45. Our separation from love is the only problem. From that one problem all other problems come. You can't be pushed away from love; you are the one who does the pushing.

46. Rejecting love is the cause of pain. And to then reject the pain is to reject yourself.

47. Pain is not real.

48. God does not recognize separation, therefore God does not punish, since all punishment is a form of separation.

49. Your mind is not in your body; this whole world is a creation of your mind.

50. Unworthiness stops us from choosing to go home.

51. Not feeling good inside is a signal that a lesson in happiness is available to be learned.

52. Intuition is a purer, more reliable form of thought.

53. Three basic thought modes come from the fractured mind: the Builder, the Collector and the Achiever. The only thing these three have in common is that each believes that their way is the right way to think.

54. All thinking that is not inspired, intuitive, instinctive, or creative comes from personality.

55. Doubt is the epitome of thinking.

56. Thoughts from the fractured mind reflect a resistance to love and happiness. They actually block out thoughts from the peaceful mind.

57. Fear of love is the greatest of all fears.

58. Process is the interconnectedness of all manifest energies. Accountability reveals the process.

59. God never changes his/her mind about you.

60. If you are driven by a need to pay off guilt, you will constantly attract situations where you can pay off your debt by sacrificing yourself. But the debt never gets paid off, and the guilt keeps compounding.

61. Anger is a secondary emotion created to hide a deeper pain.

62. You are never angry or upset for the reason you think.

63. Purpose is the experience of peace and gratitude—for no particular reason.

64. Whatever lessons we don't learn are passed on to our children to learn.

65. Inner conflict occurs when your "heart" calls you one way, and your "head" wants to go in a different direction.

66. Worrying about someone diminishes them; it states that "I didn't make it, so they can't."

67. To listen to your heart takes extraordinary patience, determination in the face of uncertainty, and the humility to admit that you really know nothing.

68. If you don't like what you see, it's pointless to change the mirror.

69. When acting out of social or family obligation, the action brings no fulfillment, but you would feel too guilty to stop.

70. Giving from the heart is its own reward. You know that you're truly giving when you are not attached to the results.

71. You are us.

72.   In all relationship conflicts, both parties are feeling the exact same feeling simultaneously, but approaching it from different viewpoints.

73.   The world is one big classroom—its only curriculum is to teach you how to hear and respond to the call to *come home.*

74.   Linear time is only one way of perceiving time. In the deeper level of the mind, the past and the future are happening now.

75.   Linear time, like rational, logical, and analytical thought, is the ego's invention to prove that fear, guilt and separation are the truth.

If you would like to write to Christopher, or to find out more information on his **Leadership Training Programs, Workshops, Seminars,** or other material concerning his work, please write to:

Box 5
Nelson, British Columbia
Canada
V1L 5P7

Printed on paper
containing over 50%
recycled paper including
10% post-consumer fibre.

Printed and bound in Canada by
Best Gagné Book Manufacturers